City of
Disciples

KILLER WORDS PUBLISHING
Cover art by C. L. Conolly

CITY OF DISCIPLES
ISBN - 978-0-9886876-7-7

C. L. Conolly
www.clconolly.com
New Ulm, Texas

Printed in the United States of America

10 9 8 7 6 5 4 3 2 1

City of Disciples

C. L. Conolly

Also written by C. L. Conolly

<u>The Affair Series</u>
Forbidden Affair
Family Affair
Fundamental Affair
Fruitful Affair

<u>Single Titles</u>
Friendly Misfortunes
Killer Suburbia

<u>Cult Series</u>
Disciples Doctrine
City of Disciples
Shunning of Disciples-(fall 2023)
Mutiny of Disciples-(early 2024)
Disbanding of Disciples-(summer 2024)

Live your life with tolerance,
equality and acceptance of all disciples.

One

The first day in the religious studies class Azril thought about how overly religious people, in all denominations, seem to twist the teachings of the God they serve in order to benefit them. Then, they go out and preach the word of their God to others and if those they preach to don't want to join their religion, they are mocked and ridiculed.

There wasn't a single religion Azril had learned

about that didn't have a large group of people who would most likely beat someone to death for having different beliefs. That is, of course, if it was legal. In the Bible, beating and stoning was a regular practice in the Old Testament. Even certain countries in the world still have barbaric torture methods inflicted upon its citizens, with public humiliation... all in the name of God.

Azril grew up as a Christian. He was forced to go to church each week, as well as sit with his mother daily for bible study. Quite a few of the parishioners at the church would stand around, Sunday morning, after the service and gossip about others. There were also several services where he felt as though the pastor himself was being less than accepting of people who were different, or lived a different lifestyle.

Sure there was a bible to live by, but it was written in a different time and the world had evolved. The Bible also teaches acceptance and love thy neighbor. Most Christians believe if people don't follow the Bible to the letter, in the way it is translated to them, then those people aren't deserving of their time. Yet those are the same Christians who are two faced and don't follow the Bible to the letter themselves because they preach Jesus died for their sins and everyone is forgiven, no matter what horrendous act they have committed.

Even though they weren't enrolled at the college, Azril and Omegra were able to blend in with the students. The professor of the religious studies class didn't even notice that there were two extra students in his lecture. They met up with the few students they got to know when all they were doing, at first, was re-con and they were able to enter the class as if they were suppose to be there.

After the first class, Azril was sad that the majority of those who follow God believe that as long as they pray to Jesus, confess their sins and put all their worries onto Him, they are allowed to be awful people. None of them face any consequences for their actions. They can be shitty to everyone they don't agree with and still go to heaven and be with God.

Beatrice, a girl from the class, had followed the leader and his connected partner out of the lecture hall. "Azril, are you okay?"

Beatrice had long brown hair and wore way too much makeup. Her fake tan gave her an orange hue to her skin tone. She was wearing a tee shirt that she had cut the sleeves from, as well as cropped it in order to expose her midriff. The jeans she was wearing sat low on her hips, exposing two strings pulled up onto her hips as she showed off the fact that she was wearing thong underwear.

"Do you ever feel like overly religious people rely too much on the forgiveness of God, or climbing the ladder to Heaven?" Azril wondered, as the three of them meandered across the front lawn of the college.

Beatrice curled a few strands of her hair around her finger. "By climbing the ladder to Heaven, you mean doing good deeds in favor of God?"

Azril stopped abruptly, turning around to face her. "Yeah."

"I think there are two groups of overly religious people. One group is genuine and actually follows the Bible. The other group gives the appearance of following the Bible by going to church and displaying religious home decor, but doesn't actually live their lives by the Bible," Beatrice theorized.

Azril wrapped his arm around Omegra's waist for comfort. "I have been communicating with God through meditation for several years and he has guided me to live my life which is pleasing to Him. No matter what God anyone worships, or how they worship Him, everyone should be accepted for who they are, not who they are suppose to be according to society."

The way Beatrice was dressed made Azril uncomfortable. She was obviously trying to attract attention from those on the physical land and not from God.

Beatrice reached up, stroking Azril's arm from his shoulder and stopping at his hand. "That would be a religion I would join. Everyone should be treated equal. It should never matter their gender, race, ethnicity, or sexual orientation."

Omegra positioned her body between Azril and Beatrice, walking toward a tree on the lawn in front of the main administration building, pulling Azril away from the situation. "In the Disciples Doctrine, no one is told they're going to the underworld because of those identifiers. There are only a few evil acts that God considers worthy of the underworld."

"What is the Disciples Doctrine?" Beatrice inquired.

"It is the word of God followed by the disciples," Omegra said, in a condescending way.

"Do you have any copies of the Disciples Doctrine? I would love to learn about the disciples," Beatrice said, bouncing on the balls of her feet like a child.

"Do you think others would feel the same? I'm just tired of fake religious people. They act all high and mighty as if they are better than everyone else. They are also less accepting of people who live a different lifestyle than they do," Azril wondered.

"If you want help developing your religion, I would be willing to assist," Beatrice offered, looking down and grinding the toe of her right foot into the dirt trying to be coy.

"The disciples are not a religion, it's a lifestyle. Anyone who decides to become a disciple and follow the Disciples Doctrine, will find favor with God," Azril told Beatrice.

Beatrice sat down on the lawn in front of Azril, looking up at him. "More people than you would think are still trying to find their place in this world and the disciples might actually be what they need. How soon do you think you could have copies of the Disciples Doctrine?"

Azril peered down at her and took two steps back, leaning against the tree. "Right now, all I have is the notes I have written during my meditation sessions with God. He has told me what is expected of the disciples and now I am, as the leader of the disciples, on a mission to convert more disciples."

"I have a laptop in my dorm. I could use your notes and format it into a book. There are several websites I can submit it to and have it printed and bound, in order to make it official," Beatrice suggested.

Omegra stepped in front of Azril, placing herself between her connected partner and Beatrice again. "I don't think you should trust her with your personal notes."

Azril gazed into Omegra's eyes, for only a moment, before nodding in agreement. "Beatrice, I appreciate your offer, but the notes I possess for the Disciples Doctrine are the sacred words of God and I am not comfortable passing them on to someone who has not yet converted as a disciple."

Beatrice stood and placed her hand on his shoulder. Again, she rubbed her hand all the way down his arm and grabbed his hand. "I understand that, but I'm not asking to take the Disciples Doctrine away from you. I just want to help. I have never felt as though I fit in anywhere, but I feel like I could fit in with the disciples. If it makes you more comfortable, you could make copies of those pages in the library and you can keep the originals."

Azril pulled his hand away from Beatrice and wrapped his arms around Omegra's shoulders, embracing her. "What do you think about that idea?"

"That's better than leaving us without a copy in the City of Disciples and she won't have the original," Omegra whispered in his ear.

"Okay. Beatrice, I'm going to trust you with a copy, but keep in mind, reporting false information is one of the evil acts in the Disciples Doctrine," Azril told her. "Where is the library, so I can make the copies?"

Beatrice led both Azril and Omegra toward the campus library. They walked through the front doors and headed to the left. There were several copy machines lined up along the wall. They stepped up to the first machine and Azril pulled the pages of the Disciples Doctrine from his backpack.

He passed the pages to Omegra and she placed them one by one on the glass and made the copies. As Azril observed his connected partner, Beatrice leaned in close behind him, taking in his musky scent. He could feel her breath on the back of his neck.

Azril turned around, while Omegra finished the copies and peered at Beatrice. She was standing so close to him, he had to pull his head back before speaking. "How long will it take you to get at least a hundred copies, so I can begin recruiting disciples?"

"It shouldn't take me too long to get it typed and formatted, however it will take a couple weeks before the order will be delivered. Now, I may have an option to get a hundred, if you're okay with temporary books until the professional order comes in." Beatrice informed.

"That's perfect. I would like to have one hundred copies of the Disciples Doctrine ready to go by tomorrow. I'm planning a kerfuffle in class tomorrow in order to pique the interest of the other students. Anyone who wants to learn more, should be able to get a copy of the Disciples Doctrine after they have listened to me preach about the disciples," Azril told Beatrice, as Omegra organized the copied pages.

As Azril took the original pages of the Disciples Doctrine and put them back into his bag, Omegra handed the copies to Beatrice. Azril and Omegra started heading out of the building, when Beatrice grabbed Azril's hand.

"Would you want to come back to my dorm room for a little while, just to make sure you like the format?" Beatrice asked.

"Put it together and get it done and I will be back tomorrow morning to check it out," Azril told her, pulling his hand away.

Omegra placed her left hand against Azril's right butt cheek and lightly squeezed. He turned to look into the face of his connected partner. Omegra licked her lips and raised her eyebrows.

Azril touched Beatrice on her shoulder, thanked her for her assistance with the Disciples

Doctrine, then wrapped his arm tightly around Omegra's waist. He ushered his connected partner out of the building and across the lawn of the college, as they headed back to the City of Disciples.

Two

When Azril and Omegra returned to the college the next day, they still had hours before the religious studies class began. There were a few students heading off to their early morning classes. Azril and Omegra walked over to the block of dorm buildings.

Each building required a key card for entry, so the leader and his connected partner sat and cuddled under a tree, facing the buildings. It was only a few minutes before Beatrice emerged from one of the buildings. Azril and Omegra stood and approached their first disciple.

"Were you able to finish it?" Azril asked Beatrice.

Beatrice beckoned for the two of them to come into her dorm building as she stood in the doorway. As they joined her in the building, she began explaining her progress. "Well, I had a hard time starting it at first because it was more like a journal than an actual bible."

"It just needed to be copied exactly as written. It is the Disciples Doctrine, not a bible," Omegra snapped at Beatrice.

When they arrived at her dorm room, Beatrice placed her hand on the doorknob and turned to face them. "I only copied down the parts that were God's message without the actual journal style."

"You were instructed to copy it as is, not to change anything about it. Azril is the leader of the disciples and wrote down what God told him. That is what is to be in the Disciples Doctrine," Omegra explained to Beatrice.

"Okay, I got it," Beatrice said, rolling her eyes as she opened the door to her dorm room.

Beatrice walked across the room and sat

down at her desk. Azril closed the door behind him, before he stepped up behind Omegra, who stood off to the right of Beatrice, typing on the keyboard of her laptop. She was adding the parts that she had missed before. Omegra could tell that Beatrice had admiration for Azril. She wasn't sure if the admiration was attraction for Azril himself, or if it was just adoration for the leader of the disciples.

"It is done. I will print you a copy first, just so you can approve it before I submit it to the printer to have it bound as a book," Beatrice told Azril.

"Thank you. Now, if you want to be a disciple, you need to do exactly what you are told to do as suggested by the leader and not do it the way you want to do it," Omegra scolded Beatrice.

"Omegra, I appreciate your loyalty, but remember the disciples are all inclusive and everyone is equal. Don't shame Beatrice for thinking she was doing the right thing," Azril gently explained to his connected partner, grazing the back of his fingers against her cheek.

The leader's connected partner reached up, grabbed his hand and nuzzled her face against it. "Oh Azril, You are so right. Please forgive me."

"Beatrice," Azril began, turning toward the disciple after slowly and lovingly pressing his lips against his connected partner's lips. "Let me see what you have, so it can be submitted and you can get a hundred ready for the worship service this afternoon. You also need to be in the religious studies class, so you can assist with the contradiction of the professor."

"I will submit it as soon as you approve these printed pages," Beatrice said, handing the final copy of the Disciples Doctrine to Azril.

Azril looked over the pages and compared them to the original that he was still in possession of. As he scanned each page with his eyes, he would pass them to Omegra, so she could also view it. Beatrice may not have done what was asked at first, but she was able to fix it and the Disciples Doctrine was going to be shared with the outsiders. The leader was happy with what was presented to him. He gave the disciple his approval, before he wrapped his arm around Omegra's waist and led her out of the room.

"Azril," Beatrice said, before the leader and his connected partner were out of ear shot. "I noticed that there was a section in the Disciples Doctrine where a disciple could offer themself to the leader."

"That is an option," Azril responded.

"But isn't that only for those disciples after their thirtieth year?" Omegra retorted.

"Technically, a disciple can offer themself at

any point, as long as they don't have a connected partner," Azril corrected.

Beatrice smiled slyly at Omegra, before standing in front of Azril right in the doorway of her dorm room. "As I stand before the great leader of the City of Disciples, I offer myself to you as a companion. I do not feel as though anyone is worthy to me as a connected partner. As the leader of the City of Disciples, it is to your discretion as to whether I am worthy. I am willing to be at your beck and call and do everything you ask of me. Shall I not succeed as a companion, I do hope that I am still worthy of being a disciple who is able to remain within the City of Disciples. Please great leader, take my offering and fill my heart with the love of God."

"You aren't even on the same level as the leader in order to offer yourself as his companion," Omegra told her, raising her eyebrows.

"It's okay, sweetheart," Azril told Omegra, before responding to Beatrice. "Omegra was chosen for me by God. I will give your offer consideration, as well as consult God with the option. Be aware that this is not an offer to be my connected partner, as that has already been filled. You are only offered as a companion and you also must get along with Omegra."

"I understand that, leader. I appreciate the opportunity to become your companion," Beatrice said, kneeling in front of Azril.

The entire offering interaction took place in the doorway of Beatrice's dorm room. A crowd had gathered behind Azril and Omegra in the hall. The leader and his connected partner turned and walked down the hallway, as if they were royalty. Beatrice was left in her doorway, on her knees. Since there was still about an hour before the religious studies class started, Azril and Omegra decided to find an isolated place where they could participate in connected partner activities.

There was a building at the back of the campus that seemed to be vacant. No one was walking around it and when Azril opened the door, no one was inside. It appeared to be some kind of maintenance storage, but they were lucky enough to find a single cot in the corner of the room. Omegra walked over to the cot, stripping her clothes off on the way, as Azril closed and locked the door.

"Oh great leader of the disciples, as God has chosen me to be your connected partner here on the physical land, please allow me to assist you with filling the City of Disciples through procreation," Omegra said, as Azril exposed himself to her.

"My connected partner, chosen for me by God, I am looking forward to sharing my seed with you in order to fulfill God's prophesy," Azril said, as he admired the beauty of her body.

The activity started out slow and sensual. Azril ran his hands over her body, lightly. Omegra moaned with pleasure. Due to the fact that he spent his most formative years living a solitary life, he didn't have any experience with women. Since God had chosen Omegra for Azril, he felt as though he was being guided in the right ways to touch her in order to induce gratification.

Azril had risen for the occasion and Omegra didn't know how much longer she could wait for penetration. She decided to take over the action and forced him down on his back. Omegra straddled Azril and pushed his member inside of her.

Once Azril had shared his seed with her, they were both sweaty and satisfied. They laid next to each other, exposed, gazing into each other's eyes. He placed his hand on her belly and quietly prayed, without breaking eye contact.

"We should probably get going. I'm sure that the class will start soon and I can't wait to see the reaction of the professor when I contradict his holier than thou attitude," Azril told Omegra, standing to dress.

Omegra joined him, standing and pulling her

pants on. "I agree. I wonder how many of the other students will be willing to follow us out of class."

Before Azril unlocked and opened the door, he turned and pulled Omegra to him. She took the initiative and overtook his mouth with hers. He moaned softly and slowly opened his eyes.

"That was nice," Azril said, taking a soothing deep breath, then exiting the maintenance storage.

They headed back toward Beatrice's dorm building. She was standing outside waiting for them. "There you are. We only have fifteen minutes before class."

"Do you have one of the temporary Disciples Doctrine's that I can see?" Azril asked, with a huge smile on his face.

Beatrice took the bag off her shoulder and reached inside. She pulled a small book out and handed it to the leader of the disciples.

He held the book in his hands and flipped through the pages. "I like the size. With it being so small, it would make it easier for the disciples to carry it around with them at all times."

Beatrice clapped her fingertips together and smiled. "That's what I was going for. I formatted it specifically to make it easily carried. I would like to ask you though, have you thought about my offer?"

"Omegra and I are connected partners. You must be able to live in harmony with Omegra. As well, you will need to recruit several outsiders. If you have read the section about connected partners, then you would know that in order for two disciples to become connected partners they must both be on the same level. The same goes for the disciples who offer themselves to the leader," Azril explained to Beatrice.

Omegra decided to put her two cents in. "Seeing as you are unable to recruit enough disciples in order to get on the same level as the leader, God requires those disciples to have recruited at least twenty outsiders to disciples before the leader is able to accept the offering."

Beatrice ignored Omegra, grabbed Azril's hands and placed them over her breasts. "I will do whatever you need me to do. As long as I'm able to be close to you, I will find fifty outsiders to convert to disciples."

Omegra slapped Beatrice across the face. "That is extremely inappropriate. Beatrice, you have crossed a line."

Azril's hands were released, as Beatrice grabbed her cheek with both of her hands. He grabbed Omegra around her waist. "You do understand that the two of us are not connected partners. Omegra and I are connected partners. We have been connected in ceremony under God. As you have offered yourself only as a companion, your actions are unacceptable. If you are unable to contain yourself, your offer will be rejected and you will be unable to level up in order to be a connected partner with any other disciple."

"I understand what you're saying, leader. I'm sorry if I'm being too forward, but I appreciate how delicate your words are. You are the only person who is the closest to my intellectual equal and I don't feel that any other disciple will be good enough to be a connected partner for me. I promise I will not let you down." Beatrice knelt down in front of Azril, bowing her head, as if she was expecting him to bless her.

Azril did not grant her the blessing. "Thank you. I'm sure you didn't mean malicious intent, but your behavior is coming off very disrespectful toward not only my connected partner, but also to God. I'm torn between two situations. God has approved the option for a disciple to offer themself as a companion to the leader without the promise of procreation, to which you have proposed. On the other hand, I feel that I must ask you to step back and only be in communication with Omegra. Just until any temptation you may feel toward me has subsided. However, since we are trying to establish the disciples and build the City of Disciples with caring and understanding, I'm resisting the stereotypical Christian behavior to shame you."

Once she realized that Azril wasn't going to place his hand on her head, Beatrice stood to face him. "I appreciate that. I have been shamed most of my life due to rumors that aren't even true. You truly are a different type of person, aren't you?"

"I think everyone should be allowed to live the life they are created to live. That shouldn't include forcing yourself onto someone who was chosen for someone else, by God," Omegra said, placing both of her hands on Azril's, which were still on her hips.

Beatrice directed her rebuttal at both of them. "I'm just trying to find a place to fit in and I feel like the disciples are exactly what I need. From now on, I will focus on recruiting outsiders and producing copies of the Disciples Doctrine. I will wait until you come to me for acceptance of my offering."

"Thank you, Beatrice. I appreciate that," Omegra told her.

"We really should get going before we are late," Azril said, as he wrapped one of his arms around Omegra's waist and led her toward the lecture hall.

Beatrice followed behind them, across the lawn. She wanted to get them to trust her. Azril's outlook on life and the main concept of the disciples, made Beatrice feel included. She did however, feel as though Omegra was standing in her way of being closer to Azril.

Three

As they approached the lecture hall, a few other students were standing outside the doorway. They seemed to light up as soon as they noticed Azril and Omegra approaching. Each one of them knelt down in front of Azril. Omegra noticed them as the students who had gathered behind them when they were talking to Beatrice earlier in the day.

"They all wanted to meet you after I told them about the disciples this morning," Beatrice explained.

"Wait outside on the lawn. I will be out there after class. Thank you all for your interest in the disciples," Azril said, addressing the group.

"I told you I would be able to recruit outsiders," Beatrice said, entering the lecture hall in front of Azril and Omegra.

Azril looked around the room, scoping out some of the other students to see if any of them would be worthy as being a part of the twelve disciples guard. The first two disciples that are deemed a part of the disciples guard, will basically be like body guards for Azril. The rest of the disciples guard is to ensure that the disciples are accepting of everyone. The disciples guard will not only enforce the laws inside the City of Disciples, they will also protect the city and the disciples living in the City of Disciples.

As they walked to their seats in the lecture hall, Azril and Omegra linked arms, held their heads high and strode through the room as if they were royalty. Looking straight ahead, they took two seats in the second row closest to the professor. It was the row directly in front of where Beatrice was sitting.

As the other students piled in, Azril prepared

for his presentation. Omegra assisted him in organizing his notes and finding the pages in the Disciples Doctrine to back up what he was going to say. By the time they were ready to shake up the class, the professor had entered and took his place at the front behind the podium.

"Okay, as a recap from yesterday, every religion worships the same God, they just have different names for Him. Those who truly serve God, have a righteous mindset," Professor Grant began.

"I have a contradiction to that statement," Azril said, raising his hand into the air.

"Alright sir, what do you have to say?" the professor acknowledged him.

Azril straightened his notes on the desk, then stood. "I have grown up around religion and the church. My mother forced me and my siblings to go to church regularly. I have heard not only my mother, but also the other parishioners say things that do not suggest they serve God in the right way. In the Bible, God says to love thy neighbor as they love themselves. If that is how a righteous mindset is suppose to be, then that suggests to me, that not very many Christians actually love themselves. Is that the best way to translate that scripture?"

"I can see your point. That may very well be

true. It is possible that those people don't love themselves enough to project that kind of love onto others," Professor Grant agreed.

"With that in mind, why is it that if someone lives a different lifestyle, they are heavily criticized by those who claim to follow the Bible? Everyone should be allowed to love whoever they want and live the life they were created to live. God created everyone in his own image with free will. It was God's plan to teach His people tolerance, but it seems as though religious people have taken it as a challenge," Azril protested.

"That's true. People who are a part of the LGBTQ plus community don't feel welcome in churches and a lot of them who grow up in religious families feel as though they need to hide who they are from their family due to the repercussions they could face," Cory, a student in the back of the class, stood up and spoke.

"That's exactly what I'm talking about. Those in the LGBTQ plus community were created that way by God, in order to teach the world about tolerance. Unfortunately, it seems as though those who claim to be religious, are the most intolerant people in the world. What if the story about Cain and Abel was actually an admission to the first hate crime?" Azril argued.

"Okay, I get your point. Let's get back to the

lecture for the day. Even if His name is Allah, God, or Jehovah, it is still the same Holy Father in each religion," Professor Grant changed the topic of the conversation.

Azril pointed at the professor, as he turned around to face the other students. "That's my point right there. Any mention of people who don't follow The Old Testament construct as it has been translated throughout the years, that's when the conversation has to change because it's too uncomfortable to talk about. The problem is, it shouldn't be uncomfortable to talk about, it should just be normal."

Beatrice stood up behind Azril. "Or how about those people who don't go to church on a regular basis? I went to a church every week and participated in every church activity. I taught Sunday school, assisted with Vacation Bible Study and went to the private bible studies. The problem I had was when my grandfather was in the hospital with cancer and a bowel infection and the pastor of that church didn't feel as though he was worthy of healing prayers because my grandfather didn't go to church. How is that serving God? How is that loving?"

"I can't relate to that. I don't know why your pastor wouldn't pray for your grandfather," Professor Grant said, sounding as if he were begin-

27

ning to feel defeated.

Beatrice held up a copy of the Disciples Doctrine over her head. "He's not *my* pastor. I quit going to that church right after that because I felt that if only those who went to church were worthy of healing prayers, then I didn't want to be a part of that church. I worship God from the Disciples Doctrine at home."

Danny, another student who sat next to Cory, stood and chimed in. "I agree. Why are we forced to only accept people if they live the life that religious people say they are supposed to, when God has created everyone to be individuals? If we were created by God to be different, then why are those differences looked down on by those who are religious? Not only that, in the Bible there is scripture that says that church is not a building. Maybe her grandfather worshipped God at home on his own terms."

"Look, this has become a disruption. I need everyone to sit down. Let's get back on topic," Professor Grant said.

"I'm tired of being told who I'm allowed to talk to and associate with depending upon their lifestyle, or religious affiliation. Anyone who would like to learn more about the Disciples Doctrine and God's true plan for His disciples living on the physical land, meet me outside on the front lawn,"

Azril announced, raising his arms up with the palms of his hands facing the class.

"That's enough. Either sit down, or get out of my lecture hall," Professor Grant demanded and pointed toward the exit.

Azril gathered his belongings and headed toward the door, with Omegra close behind him. "That's fine. I no longer want to listen to these lies."

Four

Beatrice followed Azril and Omegra out of the lecture hall and onto the front lawn of the building. The group of people who were instructed to wait on the lawn, were sitting in a circle, holding hands. Before the group noticed them, he turned around to speak to Omegra and Beatrice. That's when he saw Cory and Danny had also decided to leave the class and they were quickly approaching.

"We are with you Leader," Cory said, as the two approached.

"As the two of you being the first disciples of Azril, you will be inducted into the disciples guard," Omegra told them.

Cory and Danny both, simultaneously, stood at attention as though they were in the royal guard. They tipped their heads down, lowered themselves down onto one knee and bowed in front of Azril.

Azril reached out and placed one hand on the top of both of their heads. "Cory and Danny, as the first two disciples and the first of the disciples guard, you two will be held at a higher standard than others who join the Disciples of God. Please stand and join me and my connected partner, as we share the message with others in hopes of recruiting more disciples."

"Technically, I was the first," Beatrice said, tapping Azril on his shoulder.

Omegra grabbed her arm and moved Beatrice away from Azril. "Beatrice, please don't touch the leader."

"Well, I was the first disciple," Beatrice said, pulling her arm away from Omegra, shrugging her shoulders and rolling her eyes.

Omegra placed her hands on Beatrice's back

and pushed her toward the group that was sitting in a circle. "Now is not the time for semantics. Please just let Azril continue with his Disciples Guard and be quiet."

Beatrice put her hands up in surrender, so Omegra would leave her alone. When the leader's connected partner stepped up next to him and faced the two disciples guard, Beatrice stepped up behind them. Cory and Danny rose to their feet and stood at attention in front of Azril and Omegra.

Cory took his place next to Azril, as Danny stepped up next to Omegra and Beatrice trailed behind them like a shadow. The leader, his connected partner and the three disciples approached the awaiting group in order for Azril to preach the message of God as told in the Disciples Doctrine to those thinking about converting.

"Thank you followers in joining me to hear about the disciples. The more disciples we have to spread the message of tolerance, equality and acceptance, as told in the Disciples Doctrine, the more Disciples there will be in the promised land," Azril told them.

The group applauded and reached out for Azril to touch their hands, as if he was a celebrity. The leader place his hand on the top of each of their heads for a blessing, as he walked past them.

Azril chose a high spot on the lawn and sat down as if he was going to meditate. He placed his arms in a way so everyone could see the mark of the leader on his right forearm. Omegra sat down next to him with Cory and Danny standing at their posts behind the leader and his connected partner. Beatrice joined the crowd and they all sat facing him, eager to hear what he had to say.

The leader looked out and counted twelve people - including Beatrice - sitting in front of him. "God has chosen me as the leader of the disciples. All of you have taken the first step here on the physical land in order to join God in the promised land. Right now, I need each of you to purchase a copy of the Disciples Doctrine and familiarize yourselves with the message. Tomorrow, I want each of you to bring someone to the group who would benefit from the message of God as told in the Disciples Doctrine. Beatrice will be able to get you a copy of the Disciples Doctrine. However, if you have any questions currently, I am happy to speak with you. Thank you all for joining me."

"Is this the best way that we can recruit new disciples?" Cory asked Omegra, as she stood up to join the disciples guard behind Azril.

"Right now, we want to start small. If the message from the Disciples Doctrine reaches enough people here at the college, they can help with assisting the leader to spread the message to more people. It could start in each of their home cities, then to the states and from there, other countries," Omegra stated, optimistically.

As the group moved closer to Azril, Beatrice skittered off to her dorm room to collect the copies of Disciples Doctrine she had put together for the new disciples. There was only a dozen at his first gathering, but Azril felt enlightened by God being able to share the Disciples Doctrine with others.

"Before you receive your copy of the Disciples Doctrine, do any of you have any questions about becoming a disciple?" Azril asked.

A blonde follower with a short pixie cut and dark roots positioned herself up onto her knees in order for the leader to see her over the others. "My name is Lucy. Is there anything else we need to do, other than following the Disciples Doctrine, in order to find favor with God?"

"That question is answered in the Disciples Doctrine," Azril said.

A follower with dark red hair, wearing a tight top that accentuated her chest, also rose up onto her knees to be noticed by the leader. "My name is Madelynn. You said that God chose you as the leader of the disciples. How do you know God chose you?"

"God communicates with me through daily meditation. I was the one he chose to give the message to in order to write the Disciples Doctrine," Azril answered.

A third follower with broad shoulders, that looked like he was probably part of a fraternity, stood up towering over the entire group. "How do we know that you actually communicate with God and you aren't just trying to deceive us as a false messiah?"

"I have never claimed to be a messiah. God is only using me to share the message of acceptance, equality and tolerance. As well, I'm the leader for the disciples to keep God's loyal followers safe when they decide to move to the City of Disciples," Azril told them, softly and confidently, in order to put all of them at ease. "What is your name?"

"I'm Gerald."

The calming breath released from the entire group, radiated through everyone. They all sat with their legs crossed, facing the leader. Some of them whispered to each other. Azril felt as though he was able to settle any reservations from those who chose to listen with an open mind. The ones who joined the group just to see what was going on, seemed to have a difference of opinion.

Beatrice returned with the copies of the Disciples Doctrine she had temporarily bound. As the group stood up and surrounded Beatrice, in order to get their copies of the Disciples Doctrine, Azril noticed a couple of the students who had listened to him speak chose to walk away without acquiring the Disciples Doctrine.

The leader stood up next to his disciples guard. "We may need to keep an eye on those two. That one said I was a false messiah. I don't want his outlook influencing anyone else from becoming a disciple."

Cory nodded in agreement. "I know both of them. That's Gerald and Antonio. I will keep an eye on them and make sure they don't say anything malicious about the disciples."

Azril turned to address the disciples that stood, clutching the Disciples Doctrine to their chests. "Okay, as you get your copy of Disciples Doctrine, head out and familiarize yourself with the message written on the pages. I will be available on campus daily should you have any questions."

The group dispersed and Beatrice took inventory of how many Disciples Doctrine were left. There weren't as many potentially new disciples there that Azril wanted, but it was only the first time he had brought the disciples to the students.

He was hoping the next group would be larger.

"Leader of the disciples, would you like to join us in our dorm room? I think Danny and I could benefit from some instruction as to what is expected of us as the disciples guard," Cory asked.

"I will absolutely be willing to give the two of you guidance. I appreciate your dedication to the disciples," Azril commented.

"Azril, I do have a question about the isolation and shunning portion in the Disciples Doctrine. Are we supposed to be accepting and tolerant of everyone, but if they don't believe what we believe, we are just supposed to shun them?" Beatrice asked. "Isn't that the Bible with Jesus?"

Omegra stepped up in front of Beatrice. "You need to learn respect. He should be addressed as leader of the disciples, just as both Cory and Danny have done."

Azril placed his hand on Omegra's shoulder. "Thank you Omegra. Now Beatrice, I feel you need to go back and read it again. It seems that you have misinterpreted the message and disciples should be asking questions and not assuming, just as the other religions do. A shunning is only to take place in an instance to keep the disciples safe."

"That's why I'm asking. I want to make sure I'm understanding properly," Beatrice clarified.

"It is very clearly written in the Disciples Doctrine. Go back over it and if you still have questions, I will be able to answer them," Omegra told her.

Beatrice placed her hands on her hips. "So I won't be able to get my questions answered directly from the leader?"

"There is a chain of command within the disciples. The leader should only have to communicate with his connected partner and the disciples guard. Should you have any more questions, you need to come to me directly. Go back to your room and slowly read over isolation and shunning. If you still have the same concerns, I will help you get through that," Omegra stated, condescendingly.

Beatrice rolled her eyes, as she turned and walked away. Azril and Omegra walked with the disciples guard to their dorm room.

As they stepped into the room, Azril explained what was expected of the disciples guard. "The two of you are the head of the disciples guard. Technically, that just means you are the two who are at the top of the chain of command. Anything that is brought to you, you are to decide whether or not it is important enough to bring to my attention."

"We hope to live up to your expectations, great

leader of the disciples," Cory responded.

"I would also like to appoint the two of you to assist with recruiting the other ten disciples guard. Those that you recruit, must be willing to be security for the City of Disciples and not be shy to bring atrocious ideologies to light being spoken by the disciples living in the City of Disciples," Azril instructed.

"I know of about five people that would be perfect. I will bring it to their attention and have them join us for a worship service on the lawn before they agree to the position," Cory informed the leader.

"How about the two of you come to the City of Disciples with us tonight? Y'all can see the way the disciples are expected to live, in order to pass that information on to the other disciples guard," Omegra suggested.

"That would be a great idea. It could give us more of an idea of what to expect, as well as more of an understanding of what is expected of the disciples," Cory agreed.

Danny grabbed a duffle bag and began packing several things to take with him. "I'm in. I would love to see the City of Disciples."

Cory placed his hand on his fellow head disciples guard's shoulder, stopping him. "I don't think you understand the commitment you are about to make. In the Disciples Doctrine, it states that each disciple will need to purge their lives of all of the things they acquired during their time as an outsider. You will be issued a uniform and you won't need these clothes. Everything will have to be sold and the funds you have accumulated during your time as an outsider will be sacrificed to the leader in order to maintain the City of Disciples."

Azril looked over at Cory. "I'm curious as to how you would know that. The Disciples Doctrine were just passed out today."

"Yesterday, when you were talking to Beatrice about it. I was following y'all around. When the two of you left, I went into her room and asked her who you were. When she told me that you were the leader of the disciples and she had been appointed as your companion to put together the Disciples Doctrine, I asked her if I could look it over," Cory admitted.

Azril reached up and placed his hand on Cory's head. "I admire your loyalty."

"I have a vehicle we can all fit in. If you would like, I can drive us all to the City of Disciples," Cory offered.

"I would appreciate that. I would also like the two of you to be by my side as my personal body guards," Azril told them, just before the four of them exited the dorm room.

"I am willing to accept the position. I hope I am able to meet your expectations and find favor with God," Cory said, as they approached his vehicle.

"I'm willing to take the position. I am just a little attached to the things I have gathered here as an outsider. I'm sure I will come to be able to give it all up in order to find favor with God," Danny told him, once they were on their way to the City of Disciples.

Five

The next morning, Cory and Danny were both standing at attention outside the opening of the leader's shelter, one on each side. Cory had a couple of camping chairs, that lounged back, in the back of his vehicle. The two of them chose to sleep in the chairs outside the shelter.

"Would the two of you like to come inside?" Azril asked as he exited the shelter to wash up and find a tree far enough away from everyone to drain his bladder.

"No sir. We are happy to guard the City of Disciples, just as we have been appointed to do," Cory stated.

Azril placed one hand on Cory's shoulder and one hand on Danny's shoulder, before he went on with his morning routine. While he was down at the river, Buddy stepped up next to him and nuzzled his head up under Azril's arm.

"Hey Buddy. I know I haven't been around much lately, but I am out recruiting new disciples. You could probably go with us now. Come on, let's go back to the City of Disciples so you can meet the first two disciples," Azril said, petting his old companion.

Buddy and Azril headed back to the border of the City of Disciples. As he thought about it, the leader realized that Buddy was technically his first disciples guard. He wanted Buddy to continue keeping his post for as long as he could. The dog was getting older and wouldn't be around for much longer.

"I have figured out a way for the City of Disciples to make money. It's brilliant," Azril heard Beatrice yelling, as Buddy and he approached the wall.

Omegra emerged from the shelter. "Beatrice,

how did you get here?"

Beatrice bounced on her toes excitedly, as she appeared proud of herself. "I followed y'all here last night in my car. I stayed up near the road, so you wouldn't see me, but I was able to come up with a way for the City of Disciples to make money."

Azril scowled at her. "Beatrice, if you wanted to join us in the City of Disciples, you should have come in last night. Parking your car at the main road will bring attention to the fact that we are back here."

"I assumed since you told me to go to my room, then left without me, you didn't want me here. I was going to just stay here incognito, but I wanted to share my idea with you," Beatrice explained.

"You have apparently not completed the assignment. I told you to read the Disciples Doctrine and familiarize yourself with what is expected of the disciples," Azril told her.

"Oh, you got a puppy dog," Beatrice said, bending over to touch Buddy on his head. She pulled her hand back quickly when he growled at her. "Oooh, he's not friendly."

Omegra stepped up next to Buddy and smoothed out his fur from his head to his tail. "It could just be that he doesn't like you."

Buddy calmed down and sat between the leader and his connected partner.

Beatrice backed away a couple of steps, then decided it was a good idea to continue. "So essentially, we should require any disciples who would like to live inside the City of Disciples to have some sort of specialty in order to offer their services to the outsiders in exchange for money. They could also use that time to share the message from the Disciples Doctrine with those outsiders."

Azril scratched Buddy on the top of his head. "We aren't going to force anyone to listen to the message who doesn't want to hear about it. That's why we just plant the seed in their mind about the disciples and the outsider decides whether they want to learn more about becoming a disciple."

"Also, disciples are here in the City of Disciples to work on the physical land in order to maintain God's creation," Omegra chimed in.

The corners of Beatrice's lips turned down. "I was trying to help, in order to give you a way to grow the disciples faster as well as bring in a constant flow of revenue."

"Don't you think that in enforcing a rule in order for them to reside inside the City of Disciples they must have a special skill might turn potential disciples away?" Azril inquired.

Beatrice threw her arms up, allowing them to fall, slapping the sides of her thighs. "Well, instead of asking for funds up front, wouldn't it just be easier to collect funds through a service. It would basically be their choice on whether or not they want to give you their money. That could be a selling point on more outsiders converting to disciples."

As Buddy stood up and growled at the disciple, Omegra crouched down next to him, draped her arm around his neck and rubbed between his two front legs. "It is their choice to give their money to the City of Disciples. When they decide to give their life over to God and become a disciple, it says in the Disciples Doctrine they are to sell all of their possessions they have acquired as an outsider and relinquish those funds to the leader."

Azril rubbed his face in frustration. "All disciples are created equal and are to be compensated equally. That means that each disciple is paid the same amount daily within the City of Disciples and they have agreed to that when they relinquish all of their funds upon entry into the City of Disciples."

Beatrice crossed her arms over her chest and sat down on the makeshift tree stump chair in front of the shelter. Cory and Danny left their posts at the shelter and walked over to where Azril and Omegra were standing with Buddy.

"Leader, I was wondering how we would house the disciples as they enter the City of Disciples?" Cory asked.

"The disciples are able to bring their own tent to put here on the property, or they can build their shelter the same as I have," Azril told him.

"What if we used the funds we receive from the disciples to build a permanent structure for housing? It could also double as the worship center," Cory suggested.

"That would require us to purchase a larger piece of property in order to build. Technically we are squatting on public property here. As long as no one knows we are here, we can stay as long as we want for free," Azril explained.

Omegra stood up and placed her hand on Azril's shoulder. "Just as a suggestion, we may want to purchase property. The more disciples we pack into the City of Disciples, the more likely we are to be discovered here."

Azril pressed his lips to Omegra's fingers. "Okay, so while we are in the process of recruiting disciples, we can stay here and as soon as we have enough money to purchase a large piece of the physical land we can move the City of Disciples."

Omegra stroked Azril's cheek, before heading toward Cory's vehicle. "Great, let's get back to the college so we can answer any questions from the ones who purchased the Disciples Doctrine yesterday."

The leader and his two disciples guard followed Omegra toward the vehicle. Buddy stayed close to Azril's side.

Beatrice walked quickly to catch up and presented the leader with a double sided sheet of paper folded in half. "Wait! I created a leaflet to pass out to the students at the college in order to draw in their curiosity to come see you speak."

The front had a logo with an eye inside of a half sun. It was also titled, 'The Disciples of God'. Azril unfolded the page and looked on the inside. One side explained the specifics of being a disciple and introduced him as the leader, the other side encouraged them to become a disciple. He refolded the paper and looked at the back. It had a basic reason of why the outsiders needed to become a disciple along with the logo again at the bottom.

"Where did you get the logo from?" Azril wondered.

"I saw the mark on your arm and created it from that. Is it okay?" Beatrice said.

"It's nice. It really does look official. There are a

few things about the disciples that need to change. The explanation should come more from the Disciples Doctrine and not from your interpretation. Once that part is fixed, pass out as many of these as you can and I will prepare a sermon for tonight out front on the lawn. I appreciate your dedication to the disciples," Azril told her.

Beatrice took the paper from Azril and ran off toward her car. "No problem, leader. I will take care of that now."

They heard Beatrice start up her car and drive away before they climbed into Cory's vehicle. Cory agreed that Buddy would be able to ride in the vehicle with them and had the dog climb up into the back. Azril sat in the front passenger seat, as Omegra and Danny sat in the back seat. Azril took notes and wrote out a possible sermon for the worship service that was planned for the front lawn at the college.

He decided to skim over the bound copy of the Disciples Doctrine Beatrice had given him the day before to make sure nothing had changed. He thought the Disciples Doctrine was easy to understand, but after the few misunderstandings Beatrice seemed to be having with the message written on the pages, he wondered if maybe she had changed what he had given her.

It was exactly as he had written. He just didn't

understand why she was changing the message and interpreting it incorrectly. Omegra and his disciples guard seem to understand the message just fine. Azril wanted to discuss the Disciples Doctrine with Beatrice in order to make sure that she wasn't using her misinterpretation to deter any potential disciples.

Azril turned in his seat in order to address all three of the others. "I may need to have a private study session with Beatrice about the Disciples Doctrine. I believe she may be having trouble understanding the message and I don't want her giving the wrong information to anyone else."

Omegra leaned forward between the two front seats, as Cory pulled into a space in the parking lot at the college. "I think that's what she wants. Beatrice is purposely giving you the impression that she doesn't understand, so you will spend time with her alone. I believe she is using the disciples as a nefarious way to get closer to you."

"Why would she do that? She approached us after the first religious studies class and asked about the disciples. She was also eager to help with the Disciples Doctrine," Azril wondered.

"You are very confident and charismatic. It's extremely attractive. It doesn't surprise me that she would want to get close to you," Omegra said.

"That just seems ludicrous. I will give her the benefit of the doubt for now, but if I feel the need to limit contact with her, I will be sure that she is aware of the chain of command and she is only able to communicate with you," Azril told Omegra, as they all exited the vehicle.

Six

Azril walked up to the spot where he was going to be presenting the worship service and saw between twenty to thirty students who were clutching the Disciples Doctrine. All of them were also holding envelopes, and one of them was holding a large black cloth.

Once they noticed him approaching, they began applauding his arrival. The one holding the black cloth approached Azril directly, whereas the others stepped up to Omegra.

"Leader of the disciples, I read in the converting outsiders chapter that you and your connected partner are to wear a black uniform in order for the disciples to differentiate the chain of command. I am a fashion major and have created a potential uniform design for the disciples. The first one I made was for you," she told him, handing Azril a short sleeved black shirt, along with a pair of pants that were elastic around the waist and the ankles, but baggy throughout the legs.

"What is your name, disciple?" Azril asked.

"I'm Emma, leader," she introduced.

Azril placed his hand on the top of her head for a blessing. "Well Emma, I absolutely appreciate your dedication to the disciples and your skills would be beneficial to the City of Disciples."

She hugged her copy of the Disciples Doctrine, then proceeded to hand her envelope to Omegra. Danny stayed with Omegra on the lawn, while Cory ushered Azril to the dorm room, so he could change into the uniform that Emma had given him.

As he pulled on the pants, he felt as though he was wearing the most comfortable clothes he had ever owned. The fabric was made from soft material that was thin and breathable. The thick elastic around the waist and ankles fit him perfectly without being too tight, or restricting.

He appreciated the fact that the disciple thought enough to put pockets in the pants. As he opened the door to the room, Azril stood up straight, held his head high and followed Cory out to the front lawn of the dorm building. Omegra and Danny were standing on the lawn, in front of the building. Danny was standing guard, while Omegra was speaking to the students who had gathered around.

Hundreds of students had gathered around a tapestry that was draped over the grass, at the highest point, while Azril was changing into the uniform. Omegra was sitting in the middle of it, as Danny made his way around the group to join Azril and Cory standing where the grass met the concrete sidewalk.

Azril addressed Danny as he got closer. "Where did the tapestry come from?"

Danny pointed out, into the crowd, but not any one in particular. "One of the students brought it with them. They said it was for the leader and his connected partner, so you wouldn't have to sit on the dirty ground. Also, Omegra has received several envelopes stuffed with cash from those wanting to become disciples."

Azril nodded, then stepped up onto the lawn,

walking toward Omegra. "That's great. I'm glad God's message has reached so many students here at the college. If those envelopes contain enough money for us to purchase the property for the City of Disciples, we may be able to bring the disciples home sooner than expected."

Cory and Danny split the crowd, in order to give him a trail to the tapestry. Beatrice stood up as he approached and grazed her fingertips down his arm. Azril pulled away and quickened his steps to get past her. Unfortunately, she had decided to step up behind him and follow him to his place.

Azril stopped at the edge of the tapestry, held his arms out in front of himself with the palms of his hands facing the promised land. Closing his eyes and tilting his face upwards, he asked God for the strength to share the message of the disciples.

As soon as he felt the connection with God, as if He gave the leader His approval, Azril opened his eyes, lowered his head and arms, then wiped the bottom of his feet before stepping onto the tapestry. He hadn't owned shoes since he grew out of the single pair he had with him when he left his parent's house. He stepped up next to Omegra, then turned to face the crowd.

Beatrice sat down on the lawn, right where

Azril had stood and gently rubbed the blades of grass with the palms of her hands. Cory and Danny walked around and stood on the lawn, just behind the tapestry, with Cory on the right of Azril and Danny on the left of Omegra. The crowd in front of him consisted of the few that had purchased copies of the Disciples Doctrine, along with new students willing to hear the message.

"Hello disciples and followers. My name is Azril and I am the leader of the disciples. I have a message to share with all of you. After you hear the message, if you so feel compelled, you may approach to find out how you can join me in the opportunity of acceptance, equality and tolerance here in the physical land," he began, his arms outstretched, palms facing the crowd.

He slowly lowered his arms and gently lowered himself into a seated position. Legs crossed, he sat with his back straight and his hands placed on his knees in a way that the mark of the leader was visible to those in front of him.

Azril began the worship service with the most loving message from the Disciples Doctrine. "God created us all equal. In that, we should all be treated equal. We were all created with different personalities in order to live different lifestyles. Unfortunately, in life, the Word of God has been twisted and incorrectly translated. When God created Adam and Eve, he created man and woman to procreate. These two were meant to populate the physical land with God's creation.

"Due to God creating us with free will and the option of making our own choices, there are some out there who can't take care of the gift that God has given us to raise his creation into his favor. With that, he also has created some who can't procreate. They were created to raise the children that are abandoned, or whose parents have been released into the promised land. Those who can only see Adam and Eve as the one and only way God has created connected partners, are also the ones who have skipped over the love thy neighbor scripture.

"God loves everyone, as we should love everyone. Be accepting and tolerant of each and every lifestyle. Connected partners come in all different shapes, styles and colors and there isn't a single difference between them. As a Disciple of God, we are all accepting to every connected partner of every different type, no matter what twisted ideology self proclaimed 'Christians' have as a convoluted sense of what the word couple should look like.

"No matter who you choose as your connected partner in the physical land, God will accept you and reunite the two of you, when you are released into the promised land.

"If my message today has ignited a curiosity into the opportunity of joining the Disciples of God, please feel free to approach and purchase a copy of the Disciples Doctrine in order to learn more about God's tolerance, equality and acceptance of everyone. I appreciate you taking the time to listen to this very important message that God has spoken through me. I am a Disciple of God and I will appease Him in worship."

As Azril completed the sermon, he tilted his head back, closed his eyes and raised his hands up to reach to the promised land. The crowd applauded with a standing ovation as the message he had planted resonated.

As the applause died down, he took a deep breath, lowered his arms and head, then opened his eyes before he stood up. Dozens of people from the crowd approached where he stood.

Beatrice had the box of printed and bound Disciples Doctrine. She had placed it off to the side of the tapestry before Azril had arrived. As the crowd was discussing the purchase of the Disciples Doctrine, Omegra stepped up to the box in order to accept the money for the purchase of a Disciples Doctrine. Beatrice noticed Omegra near the box and she rushed over to pass out the Disciples Doctrine to everyone who requested one, so she would get credit for it.

One disciple approached the tapestry in order to address the leader directly. "I really felt your message. It has opened my mind and heart. I feel like my entire life I have been lied to about how we are suppose to live our lives."

"What is your name, Disciple?" Azril asked her.

"I'm Sara," she revealed.

He stepped up to the disciple and placed his right hand on top of her head. "Well Sara, I hope you find your place here in the physical land as a Disciple of God."

"Thank you," she said, kneeling down in front of him.

Several others clutched their newly acquired Disciples Doctrine. Joining Sara, they knelt down to bow before the leader. Some others purchased their copy of the Disciples Doctrine and dispersed, as though they wanted to learn more on their own.

Seven

After the box of Disciples Doctrine was emptied, Cory and Danny corralled the stragglers, as
Omegra and Azril headed to the disciples guard's
dorm room. They strolled down the hall, arm in
arm, straight posture and their heads held high.
Beatrice trailed behind them.

Once they had arrived to the room, Beatrice
stepped up next to Azril and hooked her arm in

his on the opposite side from his connected partner. Omegra saw the affection Beatrice was displaying toward her connected partner. As Azril pulled his arm out of Beatrice's grasp, Omegra felt heat radiating throughout her body.

Beatrice reached out and grabbed Azril's hand. "That was great! You did an amazing job and we made so much money."

Azril pulled away from the disciple and wrapped both his arms around Omegra. "Thank you, Beatrice. I hope they receive the message as told in the Disciples Doctrine."

"I will need to get more Disciples Doctrine printed and bound for the next sermon. There is a shipment of five thousand professionally printed and bound copies on their way. It could be a couple of weeks before they arrive," Beatrice told him.

Omegra nuzzled into Azril as she shooed Beatrice away with the back of her hand. "If you need more copies, you might want to run off and get those started so he can have some the next time he has a worship service. Since it's going to take so long to get the permanent copies, maybe you should make one thousand temporary copies."

Beatrice scrunched up her face, then turned and walked away, flipping her hair as she passed Cory and Danny down the hall. Danny had the tapestry folded and draped over his arm. Cory opened the door to the room and the four of them stepped inside.

"Why is Beatrice constantly following you around? She seems to be stepping out of her boundary within the chain of command of the disciples," Cory asked.

Azril stepped over and sat down on the edge of one of the two beds in the room. "She was the first student who approached me. I thought it was innocent and she really wanted to help recruit disciples, so I gave her the job of typing up the handwritten pages of the Disciples Doctrine."

"I get it. Bitches be crazy," Danny said, sitting down on the other bed.

"Danny, I know there is a better way you can express that sentiment," Azril scolded him.

Danny pulled his legs up onto the bed with him and apologized. "I'm sorry, leader. You are right."

There was a soft tapping on the door to the room. Cory walked over and cracked the door open, as Omegra walked over to sit on the bed next to Azril. Cory peeked out into the hallway, nodded his head, then closed the door.

"Leader, there are several people right outside the room. They are all clutching the Disciples Doctrine, so they are possibly disciples," Cory said.

"Oh, speaking of disciples. How much money

have we acquired?" Azril asked Omegra.

Omegra pulled the envelopes the disciples had given her out of the hand bag she was carrying. "I haven't even counted it yet. I didn't want to pull it out in front of everyone outside."

"You count that and I will go out and speak with the disciples," Azril told her.

He stood, straightened his clothes and held his head up high. Cory opened the door to the room and Azril sat in the doorway, legs crossed, with his hands on his knees palms up, making sure that the mark of the leader was visible to everyone.

As the disciples noticed his presence, they circled around him, sitting with their legs crossed and hugging the Disciples Doctrine. There were about ten of them, blocking the hallway for anyone wanting to walk past.

"Sara, it's so good to see you again. I see you brought a friend along with you," Azril said, to the disciple he had met on the lawn during the first worship service. "What is your name?"

"I'm Debora. Sara told me about the powerful message you gave out front yesterday. Today I decided to hear the message directly from you. We were just sitting outside reading over the Disciples Doctrine and I had to meet you."

"Well Debora, I hope you find your place here

in the physical land as a Disciple of God. I see you were able to get a copy of the Disciples Doctrine today," Azril said.

"I saw Sara reading it yesterday and asked her about it. She read some of it to me and I knew I had to get one of my own, so when I came to see your worship service today I purchased my own," Debora said.

Azril reached out and touched her cheek. "It really is amazing."

After Azril pulled his hand back and replaced it on his knee, the girls turned to each other and giggled. He felt like a very important person, but he knew he was only a messenger of God. He reached out to each one of the disciples and touched their hands for a blessing, since he couldn't reach each one of their heads.

Once everyone had settled, Azril replaced his hands down on his knees. "So tell me, what drew y'all to becoming a Disciple of God?"

Sara reached out and touched his hand. "My family is full of church fanatics who are fake nice at church, then in the car ride on the way home, they would make negative comments about other parishioners. It just seemed as though my family was unwilling to get to know people if they thought differently than them. If I brought home friends, I tried to keep them away from my family, so they wouldn't see how close minded every one of them were. When I came to college, I felt like I was able to be myself, with my own thoughts. Your message about acceptance, equality and tolerance really resonated with me."

"I appreciate that," Azril said, as he gently squeezed her hand and smiled before he addressed the group. "My plan with the Disciples of God is to be sure that everyone is accepted. No matter what they look like, or who they love. We were all created by God and God loves all. He just wants His creation to love each other, but somehow, somewhere, His message of love was translated into only loving those who believe the same things as you."

Debora leaned closer to the leader. "I agree. The government has also fed into the hate and I no longer watch the news because mainstream media doesn't cover real issues, they incite racially motivated riots and only cover incidences of the public being racist. If they would cover stories correctly, the citizens of the world would understand that a very small percent of the population is actually racist. The truth of it all is the media creates lies in order to incite public outrage. I can't take it anymore and I need to believe that there actually are still good people out there."

"Don't worry Debora," the leader told her. "As

the leader of the disciples, I promise there will be no television in the City of Disciples. There will be no negativity and there will be no hate. The City of Disciples is to be a loving place. For anyone who strays from God's true message of acceptance and love, there will be times of isolation and self reflection."

The disciple sitting next to Debora never looked up from her lap as she spoke softly. "Hi leader. My name is Cora. I have never really had any friends in my life. The one friend I had as a child, liked to drag me around in high school as a prop. I was never seen as a person and I have always just allowed her to control my life. I applied and was accepted to seven different colleges, but I wasn't given a choice as to which school I wanted to attend. This was the only college my friend was accepted to and she managed to manipulate me into also going to this school. Our freshman year, she convinced me into joining a sorority with her. She was accepted to the sorority and I didn't make the cut. After that, she would no longer speak to me. I'm now stuck at a college that doesn't challenge me academically and I just want to find my place in life."

Cora's short brown hair was swept to one side and partially covered her face. She was dressed in blue jeans and a black hooded sweatshirt with the hood pulled up to the crown of her head. She was slouched over picking at her fingernails.

"Sweet little Cora. You have a place here in the physical land, just as God has a place for you in the promised land. Even though it seems as though your friend forced you to come to this college, you made the choice to actually attend. I think it was God's way of directing you here in order to find the disciples. Were you able to get a copy of the Disciples Doctrine at the sermon?" Azril wondered.

Cora shrugged, making herself appear smaller. "To be honest, I was just walking down the hall here and saw the others gathered, so I joined them just to find out what was going on. After hearing Sara and Debora speak and hear the message from you, I feel as though the Disciples of God is what I have been looking for."

Azril reached out and touched her hands. "We are glad to have you here. I will be out front again tomorrow. Stop by, listen to the message and be sure to purchase the Disciples Doctrine while you are there, to give you a better understanding of what it means to be a disciple. We are Disciples of God and we will appease Him in worship."

"We are Disciples of God and we will appease Him in worship," the ten disciples in front of Azril parroted, simultaneously.

Azril sat for hours with the disciples in the hallway, helping them understand what it means to be a disciple. When Omegra stepped up behind him and lovingly placed her hand on his shoulder, he knew it was time to go back to the City of Disciples.

Azril stood up and wrapped one arm around Omegra's waist. "My connected partner and I are heading out to the City of Disciples. If any one of you has a vehicle and would like to join us, you are welcome to follow my disciples guard out there."

They all followed him out of the dorm building. The head disciples guard, along with the leader and his connected partner climbed into Cory's vehicle. The others packed into two other cars and followed behind as they all headed to the City of Disciples.

The leader was astonished by the amount of blankets and extra clothing the college students were hoarding in the trunk of their vehicles. They laid out the blankets on the ground, just outside of the leader's shelter and chose sleeping spaces. Azril recited the evening prayer with them, before he and Omegra retired for the night.

Eight

The next morning, as Azril emerged from his shelter, Sara and Debora were standing out front, talking to Cory and Danny. He was happy to hear them discussing the scriptures in the Disciples Doctrine. The leader was hoping he was witnessing two new potential connected partners.

The rest of the group was cultivating the crops, gathering eggs from the chickens and milking the cow. Azril was overjoyed to see his disciples working together. They were working in the way as described in the Disciples Doctrine. Just as he had read off the evening prayer the night before with the disciples, the leader was able to get the attention of everyone in order to recite the morning prayer.

Azril requested that all the disciples stop what they were doing and join him, before he headed down to the river to wash up with Buddy. "Because you have given it to me, God, I will begin this day. I thank you for watching over me during the night. I will do my best to follow my leader's teachings today in order to please you and in accordance with your guidance. Please dear God, watch over me as I go through this day and take care of me. I am a Disciple of God and I will appease you in worship. Thank you disciples for joining me in prayer. You may continue."

Azril left the border of the city and headed to an isolated area surrounded by vegetation. As he was relieving himself near a tree, that was far enough away from the boundary of the City of Disciples, he could hear someone approaching. Initially, he believed it to be Omegra, but when the person stepped up behind him and rubbed their hands over his chest, he knew it wasn't his connected partner.

Quickly, he finished up and turned around. Beatrice was standing behind him, with a sly smile on her face. Buddy was only a few steps away, also relieving himself.

Azril knew that Buddy could sense his tension, when the dog swiftly walked up next to the leader and growled. "Beatrice, that is completely inappropriate and you are not allowed down here by yourself. You are suppose to be with the other disciples."

Beatrice ignored the dog and rolled up onto her tiptoes, to kiss the leader on his cheek. "But Azril, we never get to spend any time alone. Omegra is always around."

"You are out of bounds, Disciple. Omegra is my connected partner and your actions are very close to committing an evil act that is listed in the Disciples Doctrine." Azril gently pushed her back to arms length away, then walked away from her to get back to the City of Disciples, with Buddy close by.

Beatrice was determined to get the leader to change the way he felt about her. She called for him, before she trotted up behind. "Azril, wait."

Buddy stopped and turned around, as Azril continued. The dog began aggressively barking at Beatrice, in order to slow her down and create a larger gap between her and the leader. Beatrice stopped in her tracks and froze. She was afraid to make any sudden movements just in case Buddy would attack her.

As soon as Buddy was sure that Azril was far enough away from Beatrice, he returned to the leader's side. Beatrice stayed behind for a few moments before returning to the City of Disciples.

Azril made a straight bee line for his disciples guard standing at the shelter with his connected partner. "Cory, Danny, could the two of you and your lady friends please join us inside."

The disciples guard and the two disciples sat on the rug in the middle of the floor, facing the foam mattress. Omegra and Azril sat down on the bed. The leader took a deep breath and interlaced his fingers.

"Before I start this conversation, since the four of you seem to be developing relationships, I would like you to pray with me," Azril suggested.

The four of them agreed and they all joined hands. Azril and Omegra joined the circle before they all closed their eyes and the leader lead them in prayer.

Azril recited the guidance prayer. "God of wisdom and leader of the promised land, please guide us as we do what we can to understand Your teachings through our leader of the physical land. Guide us to make the right decisions in the physical land, in order for us to meet You in the promised land. We need the leader of the physical land to show us the way to You in the promised land. Guide us into trusting that the leader is directing us on the correct path. Know that each day we look to the leader of the physical land to guide us to the promised land. Fill our hearts with trust that You have chosen the best leader of the physical land. We are Disciples of God and we will appease You in worship."

"We are Disciples of God and we will appease You in worship," the others parroted simultaneously, as they all opened their eyes and released each other's hands.

Azril positioned himself comfortably in the center of the foam mattress. "I would just like to address the two budding connections that seem to be going on here. You are welcome to gather together to ensure that the connection is in favor with God. If the connection is in favor with God, a connection ceremony will be performed and you will be connected partners under God. I understand that if you decide that your connection is not in favor of God, that is okay as well. As the leader of the Disciples of God, I would like to be informed of all connections."

Sara decided to speak first. "My great leader, I would never keep anything as important as a connected partnership from you. As of right now, Debora and I are only talking to Cory and Danny. We haven't decided whether the connection is in favor with God yet. I promise that as soon as we are sure that these connections are in favor of God, we will definitely let you know first."

The leader placed one hand flat on his chest, with the other crossed over flat against the other. "I appreciate that, Disciple Sara. You are clearly a devoted disciple and I hope to see you at my sermon later, as well as you Debora. For now, I need to prepare with my disciples guard. Thank you ladies, for joining us in this discussion."

Sara and Debora rolled up onto their knees in front of Azril. The leader placed his hand on each of their heads before they exited the shelter. He waited for the sound of the disciples footsteps to dissipate, before addressing his connected partner and head disciples guard.

Azril pointed at his connected partner. "I need you to keep an eye on Beatrice. She snuck up behind me while I was down by the river. Luckily, I had Buddy with me to keep her in check when she chose to touch me."

Omegra stomped her foot and balled up her fists. "I'm going to make sure I know where she is at all times. As a matter of fact, I will also check with Sara and Debora and see if they would be willing to also keep an eye on her and report back."

Azril reached out for her hand. "Thank you, sweetheart. Now, as for the sermon tonight, I will be discussing me as a leader. I want the disciples to understand my role for them. They need to feel comfortable that the message and opportunity I am sharing with them, is the way to go. Omegra, how much money have we collected from the disciples so far?"

"They are college students, so at this point, we have only collected a few thousand dollars. Your confidence and charisma are what will make them feel comfortable with your message," Omegra explained.

"Well, that's a start. Cory and Danny, how close are the two of you to getting your funds together?" Azril inquired.

Cory stood up at attention in front of the leader. "We should be able to get all of our belongings together and have our funds for you by the end of the week."

Azril nodded. "Good. When we get back to the college, you two will be free to go gather what you have and decide how to distribute it for funds. Also, how is it going with the selection of the rest of the disciples guard?"

"I will speak with those I know today," Cory

informed.

Danny stood and mimicked the stance of his fellow disciples guard. "And I might have a lead on a few more."

Azril stood up on the mattress, facing the three of them. "I will say though, after yesterday's sermon and last night's unintentional bible study in the hallway, my confidence is there. I'm sure we will have a larger crowd this afternoon. I just want to make sure we recruit at least two hundred disciples, before we move the City of Disciples to another property. Cory and Danny, I will need the two of you ready for crowd control by the time the worship service begins. Omegra, I would like you to find a plot of land. It can have a house on it, but we need to be able to add to it. I want to make sure the house is large enough for at least a thousand rooms for the disciples and the leader's quarters."

"What about the worship center?" Cory asked.

"If there is already a house on the property, the living room will be converted to the worship center. Also, I need the property to be large enough for a medical building as well as a separate building for group meals depending upon the disciple level. I want to be sure that disciples are helping disciples even with medical aid," Azril said.

Danny saluted the leader. "Understood,

Leader."

The four of them stepped out of the shelter and joined the disciples. Beatrice stepped up behind Azril again and began rubbing his shoulders. He immediately jerked away from her grasp and turned to face her.

Azril crossed his arms over his chest, as he took five steps back away from the disciple. "Beatrice, I need you to control yourself. Your behavior is completely inappropriate. You are no longer to have direct contact with me. If you need to pass on information, it needs to be directly relayed to Omegra."

"I'm just trying to show you that I can be an asset to you. I just need you to agree to my offering," Beatrice pleaded. "If you want to be surrounded by beautiful women, I can arrange that. I know there are more disciples who would be willing to offer themselves to the leader."

Omegra stood with her back as straight as she could, as she stroked the dog between his ears. "You realize that offering yourself to the leader does not mean that you are going to become one flesh with him. It is for the sole purpose of becoming a companion with the leader. That means you are on the same level as Buddy here."

Beatrice held eye contact with Azril. "What if I create a certificate of connection for the disciples after their connection ceremony to make it more official?"

Omegra stepped between the leader and the disciple. "Regardless of what you do, you are to only come to me."

"I'm so tired of you acting like you're the leader around here," Beatrice said, taking one step closer to the leader's connected partner.

Azril wanted to deescalate the situation, so he made an annoucement to the entire City of Disciples."We need to head out. It's time to get back to the college."

Nine

When everyone arrived back to the college, Cory, Danny, Azril and Omegra headed to the disciples guard's dorm room. There was a bright green piece of paper attached to the navy blue door. Cory pulled the paper off the door as they entered.

"We're being evicted off campus," Cory said, reading the bright green paper.

"Both of us?" Danny asked, snatching the sheet out of Cory's hand.

"Yes. Failure to attend classes and inciting organized religion on campus property," Cory explained.

"The two of you weren't inciting anything. Don't worry, both of you have a place in the City of Disciples," Azril told them.

Danny looked around the room at all his stuff. "I'm not worried. I just figured we would have more time, so we would have a place to store the stuff we were selling. Looks like we will be setting up, garage sale style on the lawn."

"If there is anything you need to store, I will make sure there is a space in the City of Disciples. Just make sure it is only things that are sentimental to you. Any items that do not serve a nostalgic purpose that you are unable to sell, they are to be donated," Azril reassured them.

As Cory and Danny began gathering their belongings, a persistent knocking began on the room door. Beatrice was standing on the other side, when Omegra opened the door. The disciple was holding a piece of parchment paper with a blue lace printed border.

"What do you think?" she asked, pushing passed Omegra into the room and stepping up to the leader.

Beatrice produced a piece of paper and held it out for Azril to see. He took it from her and gazed at it. They weren't connected partners, but he was looking at a certificate that stated to the effect that Azril and Beatrice had been connected in ceremony.

Azril practically shoved the paper at Omegra. "What in the world is this? This is deception and disrespectful to my connected partner."

Omegra examined it before slowly tearing the paper in half, while making aggressive eye contact with Beatrice. "Did you think you were going to accomplish something with this?"

"No, Azril. I thought it would be nice for the disciples to have a certificate of their connection. That was just an example. I was looking for your approval on the format. I'm sorry if I made you think otherwise." Beatrice had tears welling up in her eyes.

Omegra stepped between Beatrice and Azril, staring directly into the disciple's emerald eyes. "Disciple, You are dangerously close to being placed into isolation. The next time you approach the leader directly, I will make sure that is where you spend at least seven days. Also, you are to address him as leader, not by his name."

"This isn't over," Beatrice said, pointing her finger in Omegra's face. "I would never jeopardize my chance at being an offering to the leader of the Disciples of God."

"You surpassed that point when you put your hands on him back at the City of Disciples," Omegra told her.

Beatrice rolled her eyes, turned with such gusto her hair whipped Omegra across her cheek. The leader's connected partner reached up and grabbed the disciple's hair, pulling her down to the floor.

Omegra stepped one foot over Beatrice and stood directly above her, pointing her finger in the face of the disciple. "Bitch, don't make me personally shun you myself."

Azril stepped up behind Omegra and picked her up. He moved her over near the bed, as Beatrice picked herself up off the floor and quickly left the room. Omegra turned toward Azril, placing one hand against her face and crumbled the false certificate with the other.

He caressed the other side of her face, before Azril kissed Omegra on the forehead. "Don't worry about her. I will take care of Beatrice."

"If she assaults me again, I will be the one to shun her." Omegra nuzzled into Azril's chest.

The leader held his connected partner for a few moments, before he prepared to head out for his worship service. He straightened his stance, smoothed out his clothes and followed Omegra out to the front lawn of the dorm building. Cory and Danny stayed behind. They had collected everything they had brought with them to college and piled it up on one bed, before joining the leader out on the lawn.

The setup was the same as the day before, but the crowd was larger. There were almost three times the amount of potential disciples as there were the day before. They were circled all the way around the tapestry.

Azril stepped up in front of the tapestry, held his arms out in front of himself with the palms of his hands facing the promised land. Closing his eyes and tilting his face upwards, the leader asked God for the strength to share the message of the Disciples of God. Omegra took her place, as she waited for her connected partner to join her.

As soon as he felt the connection with God, as He gave the leader His approval, Azril lowered his arms and head, wiped off the bottoms of his feet and stepped onto the tapestry. Cory and Danny walked up on the lawn, just at the edge of the tapestry behind Azril and Omegra, facing the crowd. Cory on the leader's right and Danny on his connected partner's left. Beatrice stood behind the crowd and glared at Omegra with her arms crossed over her chest.

Azril stood next to Omegra, his arms out-stretched, palms facing those directly in front of him. "I have a message to share with all of you. After you hear the message, if you so feel com-pelled, you may approach to find out how you can join me in the opportunity of acceptance, equality and tolerance here in the physical land."

He slowly placed his arms down by his sides, gently lowering himself into a seated position. Legs crossed, Azril sat next to Omegra with his back straight and his hands placed on his knees, making sure the mark of the leader, on the inside of his right forearm, was visible to everyone.

"As the leader of the Disciples of God, I am your guide here on the physical land to ensure you are prepared for the promised land. I was chosen by God to interpret His words to you, the disciples. If you, as an outsider, follower, or disci-ple, have questions about God's word, please feel free to bring your inquiries to me as the leader.

"All disciples are to look to the leader for direc-tion through the physical land in order to prepare for the promised land. The leader is the one and only financial advisor within the city. All disciples are to relinquish all of their funds to the leader of the physical land when they are recruited. Those funds are used to support the disciples within the

City of Disciples.

"As soon as a follower relinquishes all their funds to the leader, they are then issued a uniform to indicate they are a new disciple. The one who recruited them, will be compensated for growing the City of Disciples. That is as a bonus, on top of the weekly wages each disciple earns for work done on the physical land. I, as the leader, am required to financially compensate each disciple as they bring in outsiders as new recruits to become disciples. God loves all and wants all as disciples. I have been chosen to guide everyone on the physical land to live the way God has intended with acceptance, equality and tolerance with everyone and every lifestyle. As God has created everyone as equals, all disciples will be compensated equally.

"If my message today has ignited a curiosity into the opportunity of joining the Disciples of God, please feel free to approach and purchase a copy of the Disciples Doctrine in order to learn more about God's acceptance, equality and tolerance of everyone. I appreciate you taking the time to listen to this very important message that God has spoken through me. I am a Disciple of God and I will appease Him in worship."

As the crowd stood and applauded, a voice rang out from the group. "This is bullshit!" a very deep voice bellowed.

Azril stood and placed both of his hands across his eyebrows like a visor. He was looking out in the direction where the voice had come from. "Excuse me?"

"I said, this is bullshit!" the voice yelled again, as the crowd silenced and everyone turned to look at the person who was shouting.

Everyone had backed away from the outsider, so Azril could see who he was talking to. "What is your name?"

"Fuck that. My name doesn't matter and you are brainwashing all of these fucking sheep. Baa, Baa," the outsider bellowed, before running full force at Azril.

Cory and Danny rushed in front of Azril and grabbed the outsider before he was able to get to the leader. The disciples guard struggled with the outsider as he swung his arms around like wet noodles. Danny managed to get his legs out from under him and held the outsider face down in the grass with one hand on the back of his head and the other hand in the center of his back. Cory pulled out three zip ties from his back pocket and placed one on each of the outsider's wrists, using the third to connect the other two.

The outsider struggled under the disciples guard's grasp, but he was unable to wriggle loose.

"You fucking sheeple. Anyone who follows the false messiah will burn in hell!"

Cory and Danny each grabbed one arm of the outsider and walked him away from the worship area. Azril held his arms out and waved his hands, trying to calm the disciples by directing them toward Beatrice in the back.

"For anyone who needs a copy of the Disciples Doctrine, please meet with the disciple in the back. She has a box of Disciples Doctrine ready for your purchase. Also, if anyone would like to witness the very first outsider shunning, you are welcome to join us back at the City of Disciples for a shunning ceremony," Azril stated, calmly and confidently.

Cory and Danny dragged the outsider to Cory's vehicle, as he kicked his legs and shimmied his shoulders. A couple of times, Danny would lose his grip on the outsider's arm, but Cory kept a tight hold and they were able to get him to the vehicle.

The disciples guard grabbed the waist of the outsiders pants and threw him into the cargo area of Cory's SUV face down. The two disciples guard hog tied him and placed duct tape over his mouth. The outsider flopped around, looking like a fish out of water, as he tried to break free. Cory and Danny laughed at him struggling before closing the hatch and heading back over to where the leader and his connected partner were.

Sara and Debora stood at the edge of the tapestry speaking with Cora, after she had purchased her own copy of the Disciples Doctrine. Several of the other disciples from the hallway bible study joined them at the edge of the tapestry.

By the time all of the Disciples Doctrine had been sold, there was a gathering of what seemed to be about one hundred new disciples. Before the leader was able to divulge any further instruction to the followers, a campus security guard was approaching.

"You can't gather here. There are too many of you loitering on the lawn. I'm going to have to ask that every one of you disperse, or I will have to issue citations." His name badge read, 'B. Bailey'.

Azril reached out to shake his hand, but B. Bailey just looked down at it, so he pulled his arm back. "Don't worry, sir. We were just leaving."

Bailey assertively pointed his finger in Azril's face. "If I see you out here inciting a religious gathering again, I will have you arrested for disturbing the peace."

The leader held his hands up next to his shoulders. "We were just leaving."

Azril was confident that everyone who wanted

to witness the shunning was gathered. In order to ensure compliance, he just ushered them all to the parking lot, where everyone piled into cars, trucks and SUVs, in order to follow them back to the City of Disciples.

Ten

When the leader, his connected partner and the head disciples guard arrived at the City of Disciples, Azril was excited to see hundreds of disciples approaching with curiosity to witness the first shunning. Most of them were clutching their copy of the Disciples Doctrine, while others appeared anxious to talk to Azril about becoming a disciple. He wanted to reassure them that they were making the right decision to convert.

Once everyone had made their way into the boundary of the City of Disciples, Azril stood out in front of his shelter, facing everyone, as Cory and Danny carried the vulgar outsider toward him. They placed him down on the ground at the leaders feet on his stomach. Omegra sat on the floor at the opening of the shelter with Buddy sitting next to her.

"Before I get started, I would like for Disciple Emma and Disciple Beatrice to please step forward," Azril stated and Omegra stood up.

As the two of them approached, Omegra took Beatrice off to the side. "Were you able to get any more Disciples Doctrine printed and bound?"

"Yes, I have a fresh box of three hundred," Beatrice answered and rolled her eyes.

"I thought I told you that we would need one thousand," Omegra scolded.

"With the time constraint, I was only able to get three hundred," Beatrice whined.

"Fine, but only because we are going to need them. There are some here that don't have a Disciples Doctrine." Omegra rolled her eyes, before turning around and returning to the shelter.

Azril spoke directly with Emma. "I really appreciate the leader uniform you created for me. Would you be willing to create uniforms for all of the disciples?"

"I have another black one for your connected partner, twelve grey ones for your disciples guard and I was able to put together one hundred light blue ones for you to issue to the new disciples before God's cleanse. They are in the trunk of my car," Emma explained.

"You are an amazing and devoted disciple. How come you aren't wearing one of the uniforms?" Azril wanted to know.

Emma knelt down in front of Azril. "You are the leader of the disciples. It is your decision as to who is a disciple and which uniform they are to receive. I do not have the authority to decide if I'm worthy of being a disciple."

Azril placed his hand on top of her head, granting God's blessing to her. "You are more of a disciple than anyone here."

"That's not fair!" Beatrice shouted, as she appeared from the side of the shelter.

Cory and Danny waved up a couple of burly guys, who stepped through the crowd and joined the disciples guard next to Azril. Cory whispered something to one of the guys, who nodded and relayed the message to the other. They walked over and grabbed Beatrice.

"What are you doing? Don't touch me!" Beatrice yelled, as the two men forced her outside the boundary of the City of Disciples.

When they returned, Beatrice wasn't with them.

"Emma, go get those uniforms you have and make sure to change into one before you come back," Azril told her, before she skipped off to her car, smiling. The leader then turned toward the two guys standing next to Cory and Danny. "You two, stay here."

The crowd seemed to be getting restless, as several conversations started up. Omegra stood up, placed her hands on Azril's shoulders and kissed him on the side of his neck.

Omegra stepped up in front of the crowd and held her arms up. "Disciples, please quiet down. The shunning will start shortly. Our great leader has been able to procure a few beginner disciple uniforms. They are being brought up for those of you who have relinquished your funds for the City of Disciples. Please remain patient while the uniforms are collected for the leader to distribute and the disruption has been taken care of."

Azril directed Cory and Danny, along with the other two, into the shelter. Once all five of them were inside and the canvas opening was closed, the leader introduced himself to the newest members of his disciples guard. "Gentlemen, I appreciate your assistance with the disruption. Please, what are your names and what has drawn you to the City of Disciples?"

"I'm Tom, this is Walter. We were residing in the dorm room next to Cory and Danny. Cory told us about the disciples and we decided to check it out. I'm actually flattered that we were invited to witness a shunning. I was only able to glance over the copy of the Disciples Doctrine that Cory had. I'm not really sure what is going to happen."

Both Tom and Walter had the build of football players. Tom was about five foot, ten with short black hair, whereas Walter was six foot, one with shoulder length light brown hair.

Azril held his arms out, with his elbows slightly bent and the palms of his hands facing up. "I would like to extend an invitation to the both of you to join Cory and Danny in the disciples guard. That is, if you want to."

Walter knelt down in front of Azril. "It would be an honor and a pleasure, leader of the disciples."

Tom joined Walter down on his knees in front of Azril. "Thank you, great leader."

Cory and Danny also knelt down in front of Azril. He issued a blessing to his four disciples guard and they returned to their feet.

"Good. Now, what did you do with Beatrice?" Azril asked, Tom and Walter.

Tom stood up straight with a look on his face

as if he was proud of himself. "We zip tied her to a tree just outside the border of the City of Disciples. Cory has already explained the trouble you have been having with her and we agreed to assist with containing her and figuring out a way to place her in isolation for short periods of time, until you say otherwise."

"Thank you. Disciple Emma has created our uniforms and she has some grey ones for you. Let's go out here and issue uniforms to the disciples. Anyone who has not relinquished their funds to the City of Disciples, does not get a uniform," Azril informed them, as he stepped through the opening of the shelter.

Omegra was standing next to Emma, making an announcement to everyone in the City of Disciples. "To all of you who have joined us today, if you would like to stay here in the City of Disciples, please familiarize yourself with Converting Outsiders in the Disciples Doctrine. For those of you who have already complied, please step forward. The leader will issue you a uniform."

The disciples lined up and waited for the leader to issue them a light blue uniform. Omegra gave him a yes or no as to those that had already relinquished their funds. Some had envelopes of cash and were handing their funds to Omegra as they stepped up to the front of the line, but the others just seemed to herd like cattle as if they didn't really understand what was going on.

Once all the disciples who had contributed to the City of Disciples had received their uniforms, Azril handed Omegra hers and the four disciples guard were issued theirs as well.

"Those of you with uniforms, please come to the front. Each of you will get a chance to change inside the shelter. You are also the ones who will be up front for the shunning," Azril announced.

The outsider had tired himself out, as he had stopped struggling under his bindings. Once the disciples guard had changed into their uniforms, Cory snipped off the zip ties that held the outsider's feet up to his hands, as Danny lifted him up to a standing position.

Azril ripped the tape off the outsider's mouth. "You are about to witness the power I hold. Maybe then you will see how much good I am trying to bring to the disciples on the physical land."

The outsider spit in the leader's face. "You are brain washing these people into joining a cult."

Azril wiped the sputum from his face, then backhanded the outsider across his cheek. "You are going to regret that."

"Where did you want to conduct the shunning?" Cory asked.

"Once all the disciples have changed into their

uniforms, I will guide everyone down to the river. After the shunning, he will be thrown into the water and forgotten," Azril told him.

Omegra was assisting the disciples as they changed their clothes. She made sure that they were comfortable and not being exposed to the others. The leader's connected partner also took the clothes the disciples had changed out of and had them folded neatly in a pile in a corner of the shelter.

"Attention disciples and followers, please follow us down to the river to gather for the shunning," Azril said.

The leader and his connected partner led the crowd, as the disciples guard followed behind them, dragging the outsider. The group was chanting, 'shun the outsider' as they walked down to the water.

Azril stopped at the water's edge, as Omegra stayed back about five feet to stop the disciples from getting too close. The disciples guard stepped up to the leader with the outsider in tow and shoved him down onto his knees, facing the crowd.

Azril began reciting the shunning ceremony. "We are gathered here to witness the shunning of this outsider from the physical land, just as God will shun them from the promised land. They are guilty of disrespect for the leader and all of the disciples. For each offense they have committed against the disciples, they will be bled of their wrong doings before being released from the physical land. If the shunned outsider has wronged any disciple, please step forward. If you wish, you may assist in the shunning."

Tom handed Azril a knife, as a few disciples stepped forward. Walter stood behind the outsider, his hands on the outsider's shoulders, with Cory and Danny standing on each side of the outsider, holding out his arms.

Azril stepped up to the first disciple in line and handed them the knife. "Please step up to the outsider and inflict one cut to his physical form for each time you felt wronged by him. As you cut, make sure he knows how his actions have affected you."

There were only four disciples who felt wronged by the outsider. They went down the line slashing him with the knife one or two times, stating why they were participating. Each time the blade split through the outsider's epidermal layer, he yelled out. Between each disciple, he struggled under the grip of the disciples guard.

"You assumed I don't have a mind of my own."

"You assaulted my ears with your yelling and disrespect."

"You infiltrated a group you weren't a part of and insulted the beliefs of everyone in that group."

"You were my boyfriend's roommate and I just don't like you."

When the last disciple completed her cuts, she handed the knife back to Azril with a huge smile on her face. The leader stepped in front of the outsider and faced the crowd. As he lifted his arms, parallel to the ground, Cory and Danny lifted the outsider up to his feet.

"This outsider is now to be shunned. God of wisdom and leader of the promised land, we bring before you the shunning of an outsider who has gone against the City of Disciples and against You. Just as we have shunned them from the physical land, You will shun them from the promised land. Be with all disciples as we forget about the shunned outsider and continue to look toward You. We are Disciples of God and we will appease You in worship." Azril recited the shunning prayer, before plunging the knife into the outsider's abdomen right next to his left hip, then dragging the blade across the front and stopping at his right hip.

Blood poured from the lower half of the outsider. When his intestines emerged from the incision, several witnesses gasped in horror. A murmur fell over the crowd, so Omegra decided to walk through and find out if any of them were having a problem.

The four disciples guard gathered the pieces of the outsider and tossed him into the river. The disciples wearing the uniform applauded. There were several of the others who united in the applause, as the leader joined his connected partner, as well as the disciples guard, walking through the group, observing their reactions. There were several witnesses crying, as well as a few of them seeming to be hyperventilating.

Azril and Omegra led everyone back toward the confines of the City of Disciples. Just as they made it to the border wall, the leader turned to address the disciples guard. "Tom and Walter, I need the two of you to get the names of everyone who was here for the shunning and make sure they are aware that the shunning ceremony is powered by God and not the government."

Tom and Walter headed off to check-in with everyone who was a witness to the shunning. Cory and Danny stood at the opening to the City of Disciples to observe everyone who came back. Azril and Omegra entered the shelter to discuss the property search. Omegra lounged across the foam mattress next to Buddy.

"I have located several plots of land for you to look at. We can go look tomorrow and you can choose the one you think would be the best fit," Omegra informed the leader.

"Perfect. I would like to be able to get all of the disciples moved into the City of Disciples before all of them are evicted from the campus," Azril explained.

Walter poked his head into the opening of the shelter. "Are you going to do tomorrow's sermon at the college, or did you want everyone here?"

"I am planning to continue the worship services on the lawn of the campus until we are able to get all of the disciples moved into the new City of Disciples," he told him.

Omegra tilted her head. "What about the campus security?"

Azril rolled his eyes at that whole situation. "I'm not worried about the rent a cop. All he can do is tell us to go away and issue citations. I don't own a government identification, so if he asks for my name, I can tell him whatever I want."

"Sounds like a plan," Omegra began, as she stood and walked over to peek out of the opening of the shelter. "Well, it looks like about eighty five percent of the group has decided to hang around. Are you going to do another bible study with them?"

Azril invited Walter into the shelter. Cory and Danny entered shortly after, with Tom close behind them.

Azril wanted to make sure that no one was traumatized by what they had just witnessed. "As a matter of fact, I think I'm going to check in with them. Cory and Danny, the two of you know where your posts are. Tom and Walter, I want the two of you to stand at the entrance of the border of the City of Disciples. Keep an eye out for anyone leaving and if anyone is wanting to come in. Before that, I need you to bring Beatrice back over here."

Tom and Walter headed off to retrieve Beatrice, as the others stepped out of the shelter to join the followers. The crowd erupted with applause again as the leader emerged last.

"Please, calm down," Azril began, waiting for them to get quiet. "If any of you have any strong feelings about the shunning, please step forward, so we can discuss it. I want to make sure everyone understands that you are all safe here and anytime someone threatens your safety, I will make sure they are disciplined in the way God has informed me in order to protect His disciples."

Everyone began looking around to see if anyone was going to step forward. No one made a move toward Azril. He figured anyone who had a problem with the shunning had already left. After a few moments, Tom and Walter returned with Beatrice. Her hands were zip tied behind her back in order to keep her from touching Azril.

Omegra stepped in front of the leader to make an announcement. "If everyone here is comfortable with witnessing a shunning, I would like you all to make sure you have a copy of the Disciples Doctrine and familiarize yourselves with converting an outsider. Once you understand what it means to be a disciple, you will be issued a uniform."

Azril placed his hand on his connected partner's shoulder and stepped up next to her. "Thank you, Omegra. I value you as my connected partner. Now, for those of you who have been issued uniforms, you are welcome to stay here in the City of Disciples. We are looking for a larger plot of land for the City of Disciples in order to house thousands."

"What about the ones who don't have uniforms yet, but need a place to stay?" one person from the crowd asked.

"Everyone is welcome to stay here. Please see Omegra when I am done. As for now, I have a disciple who has allowed her urges to disrespect my connected partner. As the leader of the disciples, I preach the message of acceptance, equality and tolerance as told to me by God which is written in the Disciples Doctrine. Does anyone have any suggestions as to what I should do with this disciple?" Azril asked the group.

Sara raised her hand over the crowd in order to be seen. "If the disciple is useful to the City of Disciples, then they should be warned. If the behavior doesn't stop, they should be put in isolation. If isolation doesn't stop the behavior, then they should be shunned."

"This is unfair. I'm the one who created the Disciples Doctrine. You can't put me in isolation," Beatrice complained.

Omegra shoved Beatrice. "First of all, you didn't create the Disciples Doctrine. All you did was type the handwritten pages that the leader gave you and turned it into a bound book. That means that you should know better than anyone else what the message is."

Debora raised her hand over the crowd, mimicking Sara. "Maybe we could create a temporary isolation for the disciples who need reflection before we get moved to the permanent City of Disciples."

Azril pointed in the direction of Debora. "That sounds like a great idea. I will be sure to have my disciples guard construct something for that purpose. Beatrice, do you see how even the other disciples notice that your actions are inappropriate? This is your last warning. You are only allowed to converse with Omegra from now on and you are no longer to approach me. Now that there are disciples with uniforms, you are to adhere to the chain of command here in the City of Disciples. The next time you disrespect my connected partner, you will go into isolation."

Beatrice stomped her foot and whined. "What about my offering? I offered myself to the leader, as it is written in the Disciples Doctrine."

"Cory, cut her loose, so I can move on from this. As for your inquiry disciple, your offering has been denied," Azril said.

Cory snipped off the zip ties. Tom and Walter let Beatrice go into the crowd. She latched onto someone, that Azril hadn't seen before. He was glad that she was bringing in new potential disciples.

"Does anyone here have any questions about becoming a disciple, or just a question in general about the Disciples of God?" Azril asked.

"Hi Leader, my name is Ruth. I'm just so overwhelmed right now. I'm close with my family, but their expectations for my life are not the same as my expectations. I wanted to travel and go to different countries for the first five years after high school, but my parents engrained that I needed to go to college and get a degree first. I feel like my path in life is no longer my path and I just want to find purpose in my own life."

She was very soft spoken and kept her head down. Her box dyed, bright blue, chin length hair was swept to one side of her head, exposing the close shave on the other side.

"I understand, Ruth. Sometimes it seems like our parents want what is best for us, but in actuality, it's not what we want for ourselves. If you find peace and inclusion within the disciples, please feel free to stay here with us in the City of Disciples. You are accepted as you are," Azril explained.

"You are so right. Thank you great leader," Sara said, reaching out toward Azril, even though she wasn't close enough to touch him.

"Hello Leader, my name is Martin. I was born as Michelle, but I always knew that was wrong. When I was fourteen I came out to my parents and asked if I could start hormone blockers so I could transition. My parents shamed me and told me I was just going through a phase. My mother claimed I was just a tom boy and eventually I would get over it. When I argued with them about how I felt, I was kicked out of the house and was told to go live with, who my parents called, my free loving aunt.

"She is my mother's sister and my mother barely ever talks to her. She has always claimed that my aunt is a horrible person and always said that her sister hated me and my siblings. I am the oldest of four. When I showed up at my aunt's house, I realized that my mother had been wrong my entire life. I was welcomed with open arms. My aunt and uncle put me on their medical insurance and took me to a hormone specialist. I started taking hormone blockers when I was fifteen, began taking testosterone at sixteen and when I was eighteen, my aunt and uncle assisted me with getting all of my identifications changed from Michelle to Martin.

"I would like to be able to bring my aunt and uncle with me into the City of Disciples. They are the two most influential people in my life and they were the first to teach me acceptance, equality and tolerance."

Martin spoke with confidence. He had a fit physique and was already in a light blue uniform. Azril felt he could be an asset to the disciples.

"Martin, it is so great to have you here as a disciple. Please bring your aunt and uncle to one of my sermons so they can hear the message. It would be a great honor to meet others who share the disciple mindset," Azril articulated.

Eleven

Once everyone in the City of Disciples had their chance to speak, Omegra went around, gathering small groups, in order to personally speak with each person about where they thought they fit in with the disciples. Azril invited Cory, Danny and Martin to join him in the shelter. Azril sat on his bed, as Martin sat on the rug on the floor, Cory and Danny stood near the opening of the shelter to be sure no one interrupted them.

"Martin, I would like to extend an offer to you, to become a member of my disciples guard. In the Disciples Doctrine, there is a message that states I have twelve disciples guard. Your story shows strength in knowing who you are and your confidence when you spoke tells me you have authority. Cory and Danny are my personal guards, Tom and Walter are part of the guards keeping the peace within the City of Disciples, but I want you to be the personal guard for my connected partner, Omegra.

"I need you to keep watch over her and if at any time she is alone with the disciples, I want you to keep her safe from the disciples who possibly have malicious intent. Right now there is one that I feel could be a threat to her and I don't like leaving Omegra alone. Are you comfortable with that?" Azril asked.

Martin positioned himself up onto one knee in front of the leader. "I am honored to be given this opportunity to be able to serve you, the leader of the Disciples of God, as a disciples guard. I will do whatever you need me to do, in order to ensure that God's message of acceptance, equality and tolerance is enforced at all times with all disciples."

Azril placed his hand on top of the disciple's

head. "Thank you Martin. Now, I will also need the three of you, along with Tom and Walter, to keep an eye out for seven more acceptable disciples to be initiated into the disciples guard. At this point, I need to prepare for the next worship service tomorrow afternoon and get some sleep for a long day of looking at property for the City of Disciples. Cory, could you please make sure that all of the disciples guards have uniforms and Martin, welcome to the team."

Martin stood and joined Cory and Danny near the opening of the shelter. The three of them stepped out of the shelter, one at a time. Azril took a deep breath, then positioned himself in the center of the carpet in order to meditate with God.

Just before he was able to zone out and connect with the promised land, the canvas covering of the shelter flapped open as if it had been caught by a gust of wind. Azril was startled at first, then noticed Beatrice standing in the opening.

Azril spoke loud enough to get the attention of his disciples guard. "What are you doing? You are not suppose to be anywhere near me."

Beatrice's voice was wavering and she seemed to be out of breath. "I just wanted to know if I could stay here with you tonight?"

"You are out of bounds, disciple. Let's go,"

Walter said, as he and Tom entered the shelter.

"Wait, I have something serious," Beatrice pleaded.

Azrl stood up and spoke with authority. "Tom, Walter, don't go anywhere. Okay Beatrice, what happened?"

"I had been talking to my roommate, Sharon, about converting to the Disciples of God. I was able to get Sharon to agree to come to the sermon earlier today. She wasn't here for the shunning because she was talking to Egon, her partner, about joining the Disciples of God and Egon beat Sharon to unconsciousness. When she called me and told me what happened, I contacted campus police, but by the time they had shown up, Egon had left. Sharon has been taken to the hospital, but Egon is still out there and I don't want to be in my dorm room alone," Beatrice said, tears streaming down her face.

Azril took a deep breath and loudly exhaled. "I can understand your fear, just in case he comes back. Beatrice, this could have been a request brought to Omegra. You are still considered a disciple and the disciples guard will protect you and Sharon. You can stay here in the City of Disciples until Egon is dealt with, but you are not going to stay in the shelter with me."

Azril waved his hand to indicate he wanted

everyone to leave. Tom and Walter escorted Beatrice out of the shelter, in order for Azril to begin his meditation. He returned to his position in the center of the rug.

It didn't take long before Cory and Danny had opened the canvas covering and peeped into the shelter. Azril, keeping his meditation position, just looked over at them and nodded his head. They nodded back, exited the shelter and off they went. Cory and Danny knew that the leader wanted them to look for Egon and he knew they would tell Tom and Walter his expectation.

Azril was finally left alone to communicate with God. At that point he just wanted to ask God for guidance as to the right way to deal with Beatrice. In one way, he felt as though he was going against acceptance, equality and tolerance, but in another way, he knew that she was dangerously teetering on the edge of committing an evil act as written in the Disciples Doctrine.

After about an hour of meditation, the leader was given his answer. He felt satisfied that God had agreed that his decision to warn her before hastily placing her in isolation, was the right move. Azril was also informed that he would lose the respect of the other disciples if he allowed her to continue her behavior.

Azril emerged from the shelter and saw

Omegra sitting with a disciple who had a broken arm and severely bruised face. "Is this Sharon? How are you doing?"

Sharon cradled her wounded limb. "They cleaned the blood from my face and bandaged my broken arm. I was told that I would survive, so that's good news."

"What Egon did is inexcusable," Omegra said.

Azril crouched down next to Sharon and placed his hand on her knee. "I'm so glad that you are here. Sharon, you are welcome to stay and become a disciple. I promise you, my disciples guard is on the hunt for Egon as we speak and he will never hurt you again. Once we purchase the property for the City of Disciples, I will make sure you are immediately moved into the disciple housing quarters."

Sharon looked up and gazed into Azril's eyes. "Thank you so much, leader. You have a truly loving heart."

Azril stood up over her and placed his hand on top of her head. "As the leader of the Disciples of God, I am the protector of the physical land. My disciples guard is used as disciple law enforcement. If any of my disciples are injured by an outsider, my disciples guard will enforce the law as written in the Disciples Doctrine and the outsider will be shunned from the City of Disciples."

Omegra stood and made an announcement to all of the disciples and followers who remained in the City of Disciples. "It is time for everyone to get some sleep. Let's all find a place for the night."

Beatrice walked over and took Sharon's hand, leading her over to a spot within the boundary of the City of Disciples, where a blanket had been laid out. Azril and Omegra slipped into the shelter and curled into each other on the foam mattress. Cory and Danny took their posts just outside the opening of the shelter, as Martin chose to sleep on the floor of the shelter, on the meditation carpet.

Azril was curled up behind Omegra with one arm draped over his connected partner for comfort. As Omegra shifted, the entire back of her body pressed up against him. It was just as comforting to him as it was to his connected partner. He took a deep, soothing breath, relaxing into the bed, just before dozing off.

Twelve

When Azril woke up the next morning, Beatrice was standing over the bed, staring down at him, eyes wide open and smiling. Omegra and Martin weren't in the shelter and he was alone with an inappropriate disciple. He immediately jumped up off the mattress and rushed out of the shelter.

Beatrice followed Azril through the canvas

opening. "You make me want to do things to you that would not be in favor of God until after our connection ceremony."

Omegra heard what Beatrice said and stepped up almost nose to nose with her. "What the actual fuck is going on!"

"Omegra, the profanity," Azril told her, when Martin stepped in between his connected partner and the disciple.

Omegra pressed herself up against Martin as he held her back away from Beatrice. The leader's connected partner counted on her fingers, as she listed the evil acts the disciple had committed. "Profanity isn't mentioned as one of the evil acts, but she has committed four evil acts. Number one, disrespect for God, or the leader. That includes the leader's connected partner, which is me. Number two, treating any other disciple as though they are less than equal to themselves. She has been treating me as lower than her, since she seems to think she can take my connected partner away from me. Which brings me to number three and four, taking something away from another disciple, whether it be directly from their hands, or secretly taken from their housing unit and taking another disciple's connected partner with the intent to mate. Both of those last two were evident from her actions this morning."

Azril was standing behind Omegra which put two people between him and Beatrice. "Walter, Tom, deal with the disciple please."

Cory stepped up next to the leader. "They haven't come back yet. You sent them off to get Egon."

"Ugh, you're right. Okay, Danny take care of this please," Azril requested.

"I'm on it, leader," Danny told him, grabbing Beatrice.

Beatrice began yelling, as Danny led her away. "This isn't fair! I'm the only disciple who is being kept away from the leader!"

"No bitch! You're the *only* disciple who isn't following the Disciples Doctrine," Omegra yelled back to Beatrice.

Azril grabbed his connected partner and wrapped his arms around her waist. She turned around and he pressed his lips against Omegra's forehead. He was trying to comfort her. She re-laxed in his embrace and wrapped her arms around his neck.

"I know how you feel, my love. I am doing everything I can to keep her away from me, but she seems to be continually sneaking around. Considering the fact that y'all were standing right here," Azril told her, as they were standing only two feet from the opening of the shelter.

Omegra pulled away from his embrace and said, "I'm doing everything I can, not to commit an evil act against her."

Debora stepped up next to Cory and wrapped her arm around his waist. Less than a minute later, Danny and Sara walked up. Omegra hooked one arm around Azril's waist and pulled him close to her.

"I zip tied her to the tree where Tom and Walter had her yesterday," Danny informed Azril.

The leader nodded. "Thank you, Danny."

"I can understand your anger with Beatrice. She has been known around campus as a boyfriend stealer. She will find the most unavailable guy who is in a happy relationship and do everything she can to try to get him to leave his girlfriend for her. She is basically the crazy ex without actually being the ex," Sara informed.

"You should read over the evil acts, Sara. Reporting false information about an outsider, or another disciple is one of the evil acts against God," Azril informed.

"If it's true, it's not false information," Omegra said.

Azril looked down at his connected partner. "We will talk about this later. Did you want to go with us today to go look at property for the City of Disciples?"

"I would be honored to go with you. I could use a day away from the disciples," Omegra told him.

Sara felt as though the leader had scolded her for spreading a false rumor. "Leader, I understand the tone in my voice seemed as though I was just gossiping, but I promise I'm not. Beatrice is known for being inappropriate with someone else's partner."

Azril looked over at Sara and tilted his head to the left. "I understand. As for now, I have other things to deal with."

As some of the disciples headed out of the City of Disciples, Tom and Walter returned with Egon in tow. He seemed to have voluntarily joined them on their return to the City of Disciples. The outsider held his posture in a way that suggested he felt he was an important guest.

Sharon stepped up behind Azril and Omegra, as if she was hiding behind them. "What the hell is he doing here?"

"Hey baby. I'm here to talk to this "leader" here about our disagreement," Egon told Sharon, signaling air quotes around the word leader.

Egon was about six foot five inches tall. He towered over Azril and Omegra and could easily see Sharon trying to duck down behind them.

Sharon cradled her casted arm against her

119

body and peered over Omegra's shoulder at him. "It wasn't a disagreement. You beat the shit out of me and you will never lay a hand on me again."

Egon stepped toward her. "Oh honey, you'll get over it and come back to me."

Sharon stepped back away from his approach. "The leader is planning to shun you from the physical land, just as God will shun you from the promised land. You are being shunned for committing an evil act against a disciple. Placing hands on a disciple with the intent to inflict harm."

Egon laughed, then changed his tone as if he were speaking to a small child. "Sharon, why are you buying into this bullshit."

Sharon screamed at the top of her voice with tears streaming down her face. Omegra, Sara and Debora surrounded her before she responded. "I'm not taking this abuse from you any longer. You have been verbally abusive to me since high school and now you are starting with the physical violence. I value myself more than that and I will no longer allow you to put your hands on me. The leader and all the disciples have been so welcoming to me and have given me a purpose in life."

Egon stepped back, so he could address Azril. "Sure whatever. So why am I here?"

Martin chose to remove Sharon from the situation. He ushered not only Sharon, but also

Omegra, Sara and Debora away from the outsider, in order for the leader to deal with it.

Azril exchanged glances with the four disciples guard. "I think Sharon has already answered that inquiry."

Tom and Walter grabbed a hold of Egon from each side. Cory and Danny stepped up to guard Azril, in case Egon was able to get free from the grip of the other disciples guard. They wanted to be ready if the outsider decided to lunge at the leader.

Azril followed behind the outsider, with Cory and Danny next to him, as Tom and Walter led Egon off to tie him to the tree with Beatrice. "For now, you are going to be placed in isolation and guarded until tonight's worship service, when your shunning will take place. Tom, Walter, if you will."

Egon allowed the two disciples guard to take him out of the boundary of the City of Disciples. Cory, Danny and Azril didn't go past the wall. They turned and headed back toward the shelter, in order to prepare to go find a property for the City of Disciples. Before they left, the leader prayed to God for guidance to find the right property in order to appease Him.

"God of wisdom and leader of the promised land, please guide me as I prepare to find the perfect place for the City of Disciples as the leader of the physical land. Guide me to make the right decisions on the physical land, in order to meet you in the promised land. I need to be a strong leader of the physical land in order to show the disciples the way to you in the promised land.

"Guide me into ensuring trust as the leader, in directing the disciples on the correct path. Know that each day the disciples look to me, as the leader of the physical land, to guide them to the promised land. Fill their hearts with trust that you have chosen the best leader of the physical land. Fill my heart and mind with the clear eye of the promised land, in order to find property for the physical land. I am a Disciple of God and I will appease You in worship."

Azril, along with Cory and Danny, headed over to where Omegra and Martin were standing. The two of them were watching the disciples prepare the crops for the meal after the worship service.

"Is Sharon okay?" Azril asked Omegra, as they joined them.

"Yes, she is with Sara and Debora," Omegra responded.

Azril draped his arm over Omegra's shoulders and kissed her on her temple. "Are you ready to go?"

Omegra rubbed her hand over Azril's stomach. "Yes. Will the disciples be safe while we are gone?"

"Tom and Walter are keeping an eye on the two in isolation and Martin, you don't mind staying here with the disciples, do you?" Azril said.

"Cory and Danny are going with you, so I know Omegra will be safe. I will stay here and keep the disciples safe," Martin reassured the leader.

Azril patted Martin's shoulder. "Thank you, Martin. You are proving to be an asset to the disciples guard."

The leader headed toward the vehicle with his head disciples guard and connected partner. The four of them silently climbed into Cory's SUV. Omegra cuddled into Azril in the back seat, as Cory drove them away from the City of Disciples.

"So tell me about these properties y'all found that we are going to look at?" Azril asked.

Omegra pulled several pages of property listings from her pocket. "The first property is two acres with a large dilapidated mansion. It has twenty two bedrooms, twenty four bathrooms, three floors with an open concept. The kitchen, living room and dining room are basically all one big room."

Azril looked at the paper with the first listing on it. "It may not be large enough, but if we can renovate it and add more rooms, it could work. The property may not be large enough to cultivate the land for crops, but if there are other properties around that we could potentially purchase later, it could work."

Cory pulled up to the property and immediately Azril knew it wouldn't work. The entire land mass might have been two acres, but the house was placed directly in the center of the property and it took up about a full acre. That only left about a quarter of an acre around all four sides of the house. The house was so run down, it appeared as though if someone were to sneeze, it would fall over.

Cory turned off the engine, before the four of them exited the vehicle. Azril meandered around the property and through the large home, arm in arm with Omegra.

"What do you think?" Omegra asked Azril.

"It's not the right one. God isn't giving me the connection to this property as the City of Disciples," he told her.

"I feel the same way. It's not right," Omegra agreed.

"Please tell me the other properties are bigger?" Azril wanted to know.

"Yes they are. I just started with the smallest and we are moving up to the biggest," Cory informed him.

"Alright, let's go. Omegra tell me about the

next one," Azril requested, as they all headed back to the vehicle.

The second property was five acres with two homes. The main house was four bedrooms, two bathrooms and the guest house was basically like a studio apartment. Cory had ideas for expanding the main house, but God was guiding Azril to choose the right property and that wasn't it.

They moved on to the third property, which was ten acres. At that point, Azril felt as though they were moving in the right direction. It was empty, other than a ton of trees and underbrush. He felt as though God was satisfied with the property, but it still wasn't enough. The leader wanted to see the last one.

"This one is on my maybe list. It's promising and God is giving me partial approval. I still want to see the last property though," Azril revealed.

They headed over to a twenty thousand acre lot. It was completely cleared of anything, as if it had been used as a cow pasture. Azril was getting a strong feeling from God that the twenty thousand acre lot was where the new City of Disciples was going to be.

Azril held his arms out with the palms of his hands facing the promised land. "Okay everyone. This is it. This is where the City of Disciples is going to be. Find me the person selling it, so we can begin the purchasing process. I have several disciples who need a permanent place to live and I am ready to offer that safe place for them."

Thirteen

When Omegra and Azril arrived back to the City of Disciples with Cory and Danny, Martin was sitting around the fire pit with several disciples and followers. Everyone was engaging in conversation and clutching a copy of the Disciples Doctrine.

"Where did these outsiders come from?" Azril asked Martin.

"Some of the disciples left and when they came back, they each brought one outsider with them. We have been talking about the Disciples Doctrine and every single one of them purchased a copy, so they could familiarize themselves with the message. I also thought that those who are following the message before they relinquish their funds could be referred to as followers, rather than outsiders," Martin informed him.

Omegra sat down next to her private disciples guard. "You sold some Disciples Doctrine? That's awesome."

Martin leaned in to get closer to Omegra and whispered. "All of the money I collected for the sales of the Disciples Doctrine has been placed in an envelope, underneath your foam mattress."

"Great," Omegra said, standing and relaying the information to Azril, before sitting back down with Martin.

Azril stepped inside the shelter, as Cory and Danny stood outside the opening. The leader put it with the other funds that had been collected from the sales of the Disciples Doctrine and what the disciples had relinquished. He counted everything he had, in order to figure out if he had enough to purchase the property. The City of Disciples had collected a quarter of a million dollars.

"What is the cost of the property we are purchasing?" the leader asked Cory, poking his head out of the canvas opening.

"Everything is all set for tomorrow. The seller wants it gone as quickly as possible and is willing to take the amount he paid for it twenty years ago," Cory informed Azril.

"I appreciate your commitment, but that didn't answer my question. What is the price?" Azril placed his hand on his guard's shoulder.

"That's all he told me. He said he just wanted the amount he paid for it twenty years ago. He said we would find out when we go to sign the papers," Cory told him, shrugging.

Azril stepped up behind Martin and Omegra. They moved over to the side, as the leader raised his hands up to the promised land, closed his eyes, prayed, then got into position for the worship service. As he gazed out at the crowd, he realized that the Disciples of God were growing and he was going to need help to build the disciples a home.

"I have a message to share with all of you. After you hear the message, if you so feel compelled, you may approach to find out how you can join me in the opportunity of acceptance, equality and tolerance here in the physical land. I see that there are several people still arriving. I'm going to proceed and if anyone has any questions, please wait until the end," the leader began, with his arms outstretched, palms facing the crowd.

He slowly lowered his arms, gently lowered himself into a seated position on the makeshift tree stump chair. With his legs crossed, he sat with his back straight and his hands placed on his knees, making sure that the mark of the leader was visible to everyone in front of him.

With the amount of new followers that sat before him, Azril began with the same basic worship service he had been, in order to convert them. "As a Disciple of God, in the City of Disciples, followers are to relinquish all of their funds to the leader of the physical land when they are recruited. Those funds are used to support the disciples in the city. All disciples will be issued housing and a work assignment centered around the maintenance of the city in order to be pleasing to God. We are going out to purchase a large property tomorrow, in order to house all of the disciples. Disciples will be given a work assignment dependent on their abilities and general knowledge of each particular job required to support the disciples in the city. All disciples will be compensated for their work. God created everyone equal and as such, all disciples will be treated and compensated equally.

"Each disciple has the potential to receive a

bonus, if a disciple is able to recruit a new member into the City of Disciples. For an outsider to be converted, a disciple must bring, or invite, the outsider to a worship service. The outsider must then approach the leader after the service with the disciple who informed them about the disciples and request conversion. The outsider must then, purchase a Disciples Doctrine and familiarize themselves with the teachings. At that time the outsider will then be referred to as a follower. After reading The Disciples Doctrine, the follower then must attend another worship service. The follower must approach the leader again after the service with the disciple who informed them about the disciples and request conversion.

"At that point the follower is informed they must sell their possessions and relinquish all of their funds to the leader of the physical land. Once the follower is no longer tied down to debt in their previous life, they will then be given a light blue uniform, with housing and work assignments and at that point they are a disciple. The City of Disciples is to be a safe place for disciples to work and live without the evils of the outside world. The City of Disciples is a place to worship God and live a life that is pleasing to God. It is to be taken care of, in a way, that is pleasing to God.

"Once the disciples in the light blue uniforms

memorize the evil acts, as written in the Disciples Doctrine, they are to then go through God's Cleanse. After they are cleansed of their previous life, they will then be issued a dark blue uniform. At that point, they are able to leave the City of Disciples in an attempt to recruit outsiders as disciples.

"If my message today has ignited a curiosity into the opportunity of joining the Disciples of God, please feel free to approach and purchase a copy of the Disciples Doctrine, if you haven't already, in order to learn more about God's tolerance, equality and acceptance of everyone. I appreciate you taking the time to listen to this very important message that God has spoken through me. I am a Disciple of God and I will appease Him in worship."

Azril wanted to make sure they understood the beginning uniform colors, as well as pique their curiosity into reading the Disciples Doctrine. He would eventually explain the disciple levels and the difference in the colors.

As he bowed his head to thank God for speaking through him, Azril could hear screaming coming from the crowd. He interrupted his prayer, looked up and saw fear in the eyes of some of the disciples, as they scattered. Projectiles were being thrown in his direction. Cory and Danny moved around, so they were standing in front of the leader, in order to block the projectiles from hitting him and Martin was protecting Omegra, by rushing her into the shelter.

A handful of outsiders were standing just out-side the boundary of the City of Disciples, throw-ing rocks into the crowd. "Fuck you, you religious freaks."

Azril was ushered into the shelter by Cory and Danny, but he wasn't going to let the outsiders get away. "Get them! Protect the disciples!"

The head disciples guard took off at full sprint toward the outsiders. Some of the disciples had found refuge behind the shelter, whereas others had taken off into the woods. Tom and Walter had left their post looking after Beatrice and Egon to help Cory and Danny subdue the outsiders.

The four disciples guard returned with only one outsider. He was unconscious and bleeding from a head wound.

Azril emerged from the shelter as they ap-proached. "What happened?"

Tom was the first to catch his breath. "There was a car waiting at the road. The other four were able to get in and drive away before we could get to them. This one fell and smacked his head on a rock."

Azril let out a frustrated breath. "That means

the disciples are still not safe. There are four outsiders that could come back and cause harm."

Cory swallowed hard as he tried to moisten
the inside of his mouth. "We will keep our eyes
open and make sure the disciples are safe. Tom
and Walter, take this one over with the others."

Cory passed the outsider over to the other
disciples guard. Tom and Walter returned to the
tree that Beatrice and Egon were tied to and
added the new outsider.

Azril walked around to the back of the shelter
to reassure the disciples. "Disciples and followers,
the disciples guard has taken care of the outsider,
just as I will take care of you. Please trust in me,
as you trust in God."

The devout disciples immediately emerged
and returned to the worship area. The new followers were a little more reluctant and cautiously
made their way back. Cory and Danny assisted
the disciples and followers with assessing their
injuries. Omegra and Martin emerged from the
shelter with a first aid kit and began administering
emergency care to the ones who were hit with the
projectiles.

"What do you want us to do with the outsider,
Leader?" Cory inquired.

"Attention, Disciples. We now have two outsiders in our isolation. The decision as to whether

we have a double shunning, or we do one at a time, I'm leaving up to all of you," Azril announced.

The disciples and followers began discussing it amongst themselves as to what to do with the outsiders. Since the followers hadn't witnessed a shunning yet, the disciples were explaining the ceremony to them. A few disciples had questions as to what the other outsider's infraction was.

Cora stood up to address the leader. "Well, we all know what the last outsider did. I'm all for witnessing his shunning right now. What did the other outsider do?"

Omegra held her arm out and beckoned with her hand. "Sharon, could you please join me up here."

Sharon, who's face had turned several shades of purple, green and yellow, both of her eyes were swollen and she was sporting a cast on her left arm, stepped forward. Omegra positioned Sharon between her and Azril.

"The other outsider is Egon," Sharon began. "He did this to me after I tried to share the Disciples Doctrine with him."

Cora turned to address the disciples and followers. "We should do a double shunning. Get rid of both problems at the same time, so we can continue to live in favor with God."

"Yeah!" the rest of the disciples shouted, unanimously.

Fourteen

Azril nodded at his two head disciples guard and they headed over to where Tom and Walter were guarding the two outsiders and Beatrice. Omegra and Azril led the worship service down to the river, as Martin followed closely behind the leader's connected partner.

As they stepped up to the bank of the river, Azril turned to address the disciples guard. "Martin, please grab Sharon and bring her forward. I believe she has a lot of cuts to administer to one of the shunned outsiders. Egon's actions are not to be tolerated and I want to make sure that all the disciples understand that their actions have consequences and they will be protected here in the City of Disciples."

Martin nodded and moved through the crowd to fetch the desired disciple. The leader cupped his connected partner's face in his hands and pressed his lips to hers. The kiss lasted for five seconds and he felt an electric charge surge through his body.

"I love you," Omegra whispered, as Azril pulled back and gazed into her eyes.

"I love you," he whispered back, before turning and facing the disciples.

Cory and Danny joined the leader at the front of the disciples with Egon. His hands were zip tied behind his back and he was fighting to get away. The outsider had duct tape across his mouth, so his words were muffled. The two head disciples guard forced him onto his knees in front of the leader, facing the disciples, just as Martin escorted Sharon up to stand next to Omegra.

Tom and Walter were close behind with the other outsider. Just like Egon, his hands were zip tied behind his back with duct tape over his mouth, but he was being dragged like dead weight. Azril was worried, at first, that he was already dead. That was until he was placed on his knees next to Egon and sat back onto his feet, slumped forward.

Cory ripped the tape off Egon's mouth and the outsider growled. "What the fuck is this, you stupid piece of shit. My girlfriend is in the position she is in because of you and your dumbass cult."

Azril held his hand out, as Cory retrieved a butterfly knife from his pocket. The leader flipped the knife open and pointed the tip of it at the outsider. "First of all, I don't appreciate your language. Second, you are the one who put your partner in this position because you have a closed mind. It has nothing to do with the disciples."

Egon leaned back away from the blade. "Whoa, come on now. You work for God. Isn't one of your things, 'Thou shalt not kill'? You can't do this."

"Shows how much you know. I follow the Disciples Doctrine and in the Disciples Doctrine it states, 'Any outsider with malicious intent, either inside or outside the City of Disciples, will be shunned from the physical land, just as God will shun them from the promised land'. As well as 'placing hands on another disciple, or outsider with the intent to inflict harm'. Now it's time to be sure you will never hurt Sharon again, both here on the physical land as well as in the promised land and you will be shunned from the City of Disciples," Azril explained.

The leader nodded at Cory and Danny, who then each placed one hand on each of Egon's shoulders. First, Azril backhanded the outsider across the face in order to stun him since he was continuing to be aggressive. Once Egon was more docile, the leader turned and faced the disciples.

Azril began the shunning ceremony. "We are gathered here to witness the shunning of these outsiders from the physical land, just as God will shun them from the promised land. They are guilty of disrespect for the leader and all of the disciples. For each offense they have committed against the disciples, they will be bled of their wrong doings before being released from the physical land. If the shunned outsiders have wronged any disciple, please step forward. If you wish, you may assist in the shunning."

Sharon was quick to line up in order to participate in the shunning of Egon. She was the only one lined up for Egon, whereas the other outsider had seven disciples lined up. Azril handed the knife to Sharon and allowed her to get her aggression out.

Azril placed his hands on her shoulders and

whispered in her ear. "If the moment strikes, don't hold back." Then he stepped back and allowed her to commence the shunning.

Sharon nodded, then stared down at the knife for a moment. She slowly lifted her head and glared at the outsider who used her as a human punching bag. Lowering the knife down to her side, she stepped up to be right in front of Egon.

"Stand up and face me like a man," Sharon told him through clenched teeth.

Egon hocked a loogie on her feet. "Fuck off, bitch. You got what you deserved."

Sharon requested Cory and Danny to lift him up. "A little help, please."

The two head disciples guard hooked their elbows under Egon's arms and lifted him to his feet. They held him in place as the disciple proceeded to very quickly stab the knife into Egon's torso, over and over, until her arm got tired. Her light blue uniform was splattered with blood. She dropped the knife onto the dirt, then seemed to zone out as she stared at her blood covered hand dripping on the ground below. Slowly turning her hand back and forth, she appeared to be contemplating what to do with the blood.

Before she returned to stand next to Omegra, Sharon closed her eyes, tipped her head back, then wiped her bloody hand down her face and neck. With an expressionless face, she took her place next to the leader's connected partner and stared straight ahead, her arms down by her sides, seemingly dazed.

Egon's legs were weak and he was being held up by Cory and Danny. He was coughing up blood and seemed to be choking on his breath. To be sure the job was done quickly, Azril picked up the knife and walked around behind the outsider. He pressed the knife against Egon's neck and sliced right through his esophagus, as well as severing the carotid artery.

Blood spurted from the side of his neck, then slowly changed to a drizzle as his heart slowed. Cory and Danny unhooked their arms from Egon and his body dropped, face first, to the ground. They stood over the outsider's body, waiting until the end of the entire shunning ceremony before disposing of him. Azril washed the blood off the knife and his hands in the river, before stepping up to the disciples who were waiting to cut the second outsider.

Azril placed the blade of the knife under the outsider's chin. "What is your name, outsider."

The outsider seemed defeated. "Screw you, cult leader."

"His name is Brent. He's my ex-boyfriend," Cora said, from the line of disciples waiting to participate in the shunning.

Azril nodded at Cora before turning back to the outsider. "Well Brent, you have committed several evil acts as stated in the Disciples Doctrine. At this time, you will be shunned from the physical land, just as God will shun you from the promised land."

The first disciple in line took the knife from the leader and ran the blade across the outsider's left bicep. "You hit me in the head with a rock."

The next disciple stepped up and took the knife, slicing it down the outsider's right bicep. "You disrupted the peace in the City of Disciples."

Cora was next. She took the knife and stepped up in front of Brent. "Look at me."

The outsider looked up at her. "Why are you doing this?"

"You had the opportunity to convert as a disciple. I told you about the Disciples Doctrine and how caring the leader is, but you chose not to. You gave me an ultimatum to choose between the disciples and you. As you see me standing in front of you in a light blue, new disciple uniform, you know I made my choice. You just couldn't let go and decided to come into the City of Disciples to disturb the peace and tranquility. I was your only family and you chose to dismiss me, just as you did the rest of your family. Why would you choose to come over here and injure people?" Cora lectured him.

"You chose to leave me for this God bullshit. I want everyone here to know that if you continue with this cult shit, the violence against you will continue," Brent said.

"You never even gave it a chance. You judged it before knowing everything. I have five cuts to administer." Cora prepared the knife, cut off his shirt and sliced Brent across his chest after each hurtful statement. "You have verbally abused me. You manipulated me in staying with you longer than I wanted. You said bad things about me to other people to get them to stop talking to me. You disturbed the peaceful nature in the City of Disciples and last, you came into the City of Disciples and inflicted harm among the disciples."

Blood was seeping down both of the outsider's arms and from his chest, down his stomach. The dirt under Brent was stained red as the blood dripped off his skin. Cora turned to pass the knife to the next disciple who had been injured when the outsider threw rocks.

"I think Cora said everything that needed to be said," the disciple said, turning to pass the knife to the disciple behind them.

"I was hit three times by those rocks. I'll take it," the disciple said, stepping up to the outsider.

"One cut for each rock that hit me."

The disciple cut Brent three times. One on the top of his head, one across his cheek and the last one almost severed off his ear. The disciple dropped the knife into the dirt just as Sharon had, before turning and joining the group of disciples just witnessing the shunning. The last disciple in line held her hands up and decided to revoke her right to participate, just as the disciple after Cora had done.

Azril stepped up to the outsider and picked up the knife. He jammed the knife into Brent's abdomen starting at his left hip and cut across to his right hip. The wound was deep enough to allow the outsider's intestines to emerge and fall out of his body. Brent watched as his guts spilled out in front of him, before he fell forward on his face in the dirt.

Once both outsiders had been shunned, the disciples and witnesses cheered. Azril held his hands up, palms facing the crowd and waited for them to calm down before he recited the shunning prayer. "God of wisdom and leader of the promised land, we bring before you the shunning of outsiders who have gone against the City of Disciples and against You. Just as we have shunned them from the physical land, You will shun them from the promised land. Be with all disciples as we forget about the shunned out-siders and continue to look toward You. We are Disciples of God and we will appease You in wor-ship."

"We are Disciples of God and we will appease You in worship," everyone repeated simultaneous-ly.

The disciples and witnesses left to return to the City of Disciples. The leader, his connected partner, the disciples guard and Sharon stayed behind to deal with the two dead outsiders.

"What do we do with the outsiders now?" Cory asked, peering at the dead bodies laying in pools of blood.

"Instead of just tossing these bodies into the river, like the last one, we should dismember the bodies in order to get rid of them," Azril explained.

"What about the mess in the dirt?" Danny asked.

"It's just dirt. God will take care of the clean up for that. As for now, we just need to dispose of the bodies," Azril told them.

"I'm sure I can get a hack saw and trash bags, along with plastic sheeting," Cory informed.

"As long as it's not something you have to purchase. I don't need any of this being tracked back to us," Azril said.

Cory winked at Azril. "No problem, Leader. It

won't be anything newly purchased. As a matter of fact, I have those items in the back of my vehicle."

Azril nodded and one side of his mouth curled up. "Good, go grab those items. Danny and I will clip the zip ties and lay the bodies out."

"Leader, how about we help with this and you take Sharon and your connected partner back to the City of Disciples," Tom suggested.

Omegra was trying to calm Sharon, as she was attempting to wash the blood from Egon off her hand and face. The disciple was hyperventilating, with tears streaming down her face, as she splashed around in the river.

"Thank you Tom. Walter are you in agreement with this?" Azril asked.

"Yes, Leader. The disciples guard is here to do the heavy lifting," Walter agreed.

"Martin, could you please assist Omegra with Sharon," Azril requested.

Martin stepped into the river and scooped Sharon into his arms, carrying her out of the water. Omegra followed behind Martin and they followed Azril back to the City of Disciples. Martin carried Sharon the whole way and she cried in his arms.

"Martin, take Sharon and Omegra into the shelter for now. As soon as Cory has retrieved all the necessary items from his vehicle, I'm going to go back down to the river and check on the other disciples guard. I don't feel right about leaving them to do this process by themselves. Just stand outside the shelter and keep them safe from harm," Azril instructed.

"I will take care of them. You can trust me," Martin answered.

Cory rushed past Azril with a duffle bag, motioning to the leader that someone was approaching. Azril stayed at the City of Disciples as his disciples guard continued down to the river. Two state troopers were walking through the woods headed straight toward the boarder of the city.

Azril walked over to the opening in order to meet up with the officers. "Hello there, gentlemen. My name is Azril Zion. Is there anything I can help you with?"

The officer, who's name tag read C. Archer was the one to speak. "Well, Mr. Zion, are you aware that this is government owned property and it is illegal to camp here, let alone throw a party?"

"I understand, sir. We are all from the college up the road and we thought this would be a nice place to meet up at," Azril explained, without actually telling him any relevant information.

The second officer walked around the perimeter of the wall toward the tree Beatrice was still zip tied to, as Archer continued engaging in conversation with the leader. "What kind of meeting are y'all having that requires that uniform? Is this some kind of fraternity/sorority mash up hazing?"

"Archer! Get over here now!" the second trooper yelled.

Azril knew he had found Beatrice. Archer ran in the direction from where the trooper's voice had come from, with the leader close behind. Luckily, one of the disciples had cut Beatrice loose and he was more befuddled by the fact that there was a cow and bull of the property. The cow was in full active labor with a calf and several disciples were surrounding her, trying to keep her calm during the process.

"Why are there farm animals on this property?" Archer asked.

Emma was able to think of a quick response. "She must have wandered over from the neighboring farm. Cows like to be solitary when giving birth. It gives them time to bond with their new baby before the others meet the calf. That way, if the mother has bonded with the baby, the rest of the herd will accept it as well."

Archer furrowed his brow and looked confused. "Okay, well y'all can't be here. However, you seem to know what you are doing here, so as soon as the calf is born and both mother and baby are comfortable, you are all going to need to leave."

Azril extended his arm and shook hands with both of the state troopers. "No problem, officers. I can assure you that as soon as the calf is born we will disperse."

As soon as the state troopers were through the woods and out of sight, Azril turned toward Emma. "Is that true about cows?"

Emma shrugged. "I have no idea. I have never lived on a farm before, but I thought it sounded feasible."

Azril laughed through his nose, then turned toward the tree that Beatrice had been tied to. "Where is the isolated disciple?"

"When we noticed the troopers, Sara, Debora and Cora decided she should be moved. They took her further into the woods to hide her," Emma explained.

"Are they staying with her?" Azril wondered.

Emma shrugged again. "I think they are just holding her down in there until someone comes to get them. I think Sara said they were planning to keep her until otherwise instructed."

Azril rubbed his forehead. "How about you go in there and let them know that I said she can be free, for now. I'm going to go back to the river and check on the progress of the shunned outsiders."

Emma nodded, then headed into the woods behind the shelter. Azril returned to the river where Danny was wrapping duct tape around the ankles of both bodies, which had been placed on plastic sheeting. Cory was using a hack saw to cut off one arm from Egon, while Tom was holding the hand on that arm and Cory sawed at the armpit. Once the first arm had been removed, Tom handed the arm to Walter, who stuffed it into a trash bag. Tom and Cory moved on to the next arm.

Azril stepped up behind Danny. "What is the plan to do with the body parts once they are completely dismembered?"

Walter sealed the trash bag with Egon's arm with duct tape. "Each piece will be in its own bag, then they will all be stuffed into a single bag and we could bury the pieces either here, or on the new property."

Azril stroked his chin and thought about the possible disposal. "I like that idea. We should take the bags over to the new property and drop them off, then we could find a spot to toss the pieces into a hole. Maybe we could have a shunned pit."

"A shunned pit. That's awesome," Danny said, joining Walter in sealing the bags.

Just as the torsos were being sealed inside the bags, it sounded as if the entirety of the City of Disciples was approaching. The sound of several people arguing, along with one person yelling in defense.

"What is going on?," Azril asked, as the five of them looked in the direction of the raised voices.

"It looks like the disciples are heading this way with an outsider," Danny said, walking toward the trees where the sound was coming from.

Omegra approached first, running ahead of the crowd. "Azril, you might need to take care of this."

"What is going on?" Azril said, holding his arms out to stop everyone from getting too close to the area where the disciples guard was standing. "Beatrice, what are you doing?"

Beatrice was leading the group and the disciples were arguing with her. "I can't believe you left me tied to a tree for the past several hours! Azril, you should be treating me the same as you treat Omegra! I offered myself to you and you rejected me!"

"Beatrice, your offering was rejected due to your inappropriate behavior. You were placed in isolation after being warned about your behavior. As a matter of fact, Omegra told you the reasons why you were placed in isolation. I can see that you being in isolation tied to a tree might be the wrong way to go, so I will be sure that we will build a temporary isolation chamber just to make sure that you are comfortable," Azril told her.

"No, I want out of isolation," she said, stomping her foot.

Azril ignored her tantrum and addressed the disciples and followers as a whole. "The sun is setting. The safety of the City of Disciples has been compromised. Everyone needs to go back to the places where y'all were living before you came here. Tomorrow, I will be going out and purchasing a large plot of land with the funds that the disciples have blessed us with. We knew that this space for the city was only temporary and since the disciples have grown so fast, I had to find a more permanent residence for us all to be able to prosper. As soon as the purchase is finalized, I will send for you all."

Sara and Debora grabbed Beatrice, as the disciples and followers headed off the property to go back to the college. Omegra walked back to the shelter in the City of Disciples and Azril stayed behind to help with the disposal of the outsiders.

The disciples guard stood where the dead outsider bodies once were, each holding a single black garbage bag. They were prepared to dispose of the bags, so Azril led them toward the City of Disciples to check on Sharon before they left.

Beatrice ran back toward Azril, shouting. "Don't walk away from me!"

Sara came running up behind her. "You need to calm down and just accept the rejection."

Debora was a few steps behind Sara. "Yeah. Your offering was rejected, which means you are just a disciple like the rest of us. You can't be held at a higher standard like the leader and his connected partner."

Cora came running up a short ways behind Debora. "Just get over it and find someone else to obsess over."

"What is happening?" Azril asked Omegra, when they arrived back to the city and she had emerged from the shelter. Martin was still standing guard outside.

"Since you decided to let her go free she stormed through the City of Disciples shouting that she was the one true connected partner of the leader and she needed to file a complaint about the disciples guard who tied her to the tree. She seems to be losing her grip on reality and may need to be shunned at some point," Omegra explained.

"I think a shunning may be going too far. Just get her out of here for now and I will decide what to do about the situation later. I don't have time for this right now," Azril said.

Sara, Debora and Cora grabbed Beatrice and led her away from the boundary of the City of Disciples. The leader poked his head into the shelter.

"How is she doing?" Azril asked, pointing at Sharon curled up in the center of the meditation rug.

"I gave her a clean dry uniform and told her if she needed to talk, she was able to come to either you, or me. I think she will be okay. It could just be the shock of shunning someone she knows," Omegra theorized.

Azril changed his blood soaked uniform just outside the opening of the shelter. "Good. I want to make sure she feels safe and protected here in the City of Disciples. Right now, I think we are the only two who need the protection within the City of Disciples. I don't know what Beatrice may do if either of us happen to be alone with her."

Once he was in clean clothes, Omegra took his bloody uniform and had Martin escort her down to the river to wash it. The disciples guard headed to Cory's vehicle to drop off the bags of body parts, as Azril sat down on the floor inside the shelter near Sharon's face. He smoothed the hair on the top of her head and she opened her eyes.

"Leader, I want to thank you for what you have done for me. Egon and I have been partners since high school. He has always made me feel lower than the dirt under his shoes. I have never felt more powerful than I felt today when I plunged that knife into his stomach. It was amazing," Sharon said, sitting up slowly.

"You're fine. I'm actually glad that you're okay. The shunning isn't meant to devastate the disciples, it's meant to liberate them," Azril told her.

"That's it. I felt liberated. Thank you, Leader," Sharon said, standing and stretching.

Sharon left the shelter, as Azril stood. He was glad that her short stint of comatose was just to process the loss of someone she had known for a long time. When the leader stepped out of the shelter, Cory and Danny were standing guard, conversing with Sara and Debora.

"Where is Beatrice?" Azril asked, looking around.

"The last time I saw her, five disciples were holding her back from digging up the crops. She said she was going to make our food as dead as you have made her soul feel," Sara explained, without looking away from Danny.

"Wonderful," Azril said sarcastically, flapping his arms up and allowing them to fall, slapping the side of his thighs. "Where is Tom and Walter?"

"Walter is over there talking to Sharon and Tom is talking to Katie," Debora said.

"Looks like we have another couple of partnerships blossoming. Of course, I will need them to build the temporary isolation chamber to contain Beatrice until she knows her place. Unfortunately, due to the fact that she offered herself to me, according to the words of the ceremony, 'shall I not succeed as a companion, I do hope that I am still worthy of being a disciple who is able to remain within the City of Disciples'. I believe those words are meant as a sign of mercy to the disciple," Azril said, rubbing his forehead.

"Are you saying that because of that part of the offering, you are unable to shun Beatrice?" Sara asked.

"Isolation is for everyone who seems to have lost their way to God. It gives them a way to reflect on the wrong they have committed. She needs time for reflection, not shunning," Azril said, sighing heavily.

Fifteen

The leader wanted to try and save all of the disciples for God. He was okay with shunning outsiders, but he wasn't comfortable with shunning the disciples yet. There was the possibility that he could change his mind once they were in their permanent City of Disciples, but in the beginning, he was trying to build the disciples.

"Leader, there is thunder in the distance. I

think there might be a thunderstorm on its way. The disciples will need shelter from the weather tonight," Martin told Azril, as he returned with Omegra.

"Well, most of the disciples and followers have already left due to the state troopers telling us we can't be here. Who is still here?" Azril asked his disciples guard.

Martin pointed over to where the disciples guard was standing with four other disciples. "They have potential partners."

"Go do a quick walk around and check to see if anyone else is still here," Azril instructed Martin.

Cory, Danny, Tom and Walter were standing around with Debora, Sara, Sharon and Katie. Azril and Omegra gathered the four disciples guard and four disciples, waiting near the shelter for Martin to return. Thunder rolled across the sky, as the disciples guard returned with a couple disciples and gathered around the fire pit.

"What is going on?" Cora asked.

Azril mustered his worship voice to explain. "I have been informed that there is a storm heading this way. Everyone will need to seek shelter."

"What about your shelter?" Victoria said.

Victoria was a follower that Cora had brought into the City of Disciples. The two of them were trying to fix the crops that Beatrice had dug up during her hissy fit.

"I have space for me, Omegra, Martin, Cory and Danny. There could also be room for Tom and Walter, but the area is so small there is not enough room for everyone. With the five of us in there it will be very crowded. For tonight, everyone should go back to their dorms, but tomorrow we are purchasing a large property and will be moving to the new City of Disciples site. I will make sure on that property, everyone will get their own temporary shelter before we are able to build the permanent housing. This is just for tonight," Azril explained.

Cora and Victoria agreed and headed back to the college. Tom and Walter hung back with Sharon and Katie, just as Sara and Debora stayed behind with Cory and Danny.

Once they were sure all the disciples had left, Cory turned toward Azril. "What about the bodies in the back of my car?"

"With the storm heading this way, the disposal may have to wait until tomorrow," Azril told him.

"I'm more worried about it starting to smell. The stench of a decomposing body could be difficult to get out of the upholstery," Cory worried.

"The pieces are sealed, right?" Azril asked.

Danny stepped up and joined the conversation. "The bodies have been mostly dismembered.

Each arm, the torsos and the heads all have their own sealed bags. Whereas the legs were duct taped together and both legs, from each outsider, were placed in the same bags. Those pieces were then stuffed into fifty five gallon, industrial strength, black trash bags. Each of the individual bags were sealed with duct tape and the two bags containing all of the parts are sealed with duct tape."

"Do you think we should double bag the body parts to make sure there is no possibility for leakage?" Azril asked.

"Tom and Walter helped me with that. I definitely don't want any biological fluids leaking into the back of my vehicle," Cory informed, as thunder rolled through the clouds overhead.

"Well, you have two options. One, you can take Tom and Walter with you to the property we will be purchasing tomorrow and you can dump the bags there and we can deal with them later, or two, you can wait until tomorrow after the purchase of the property and we can dig the shunning pit to dump the bags in," Azril explained.

"With the storm coming, we might want to wait until morning. It could be worse than just a thunderstorm, or a little rain," Danny said.

Cory looked up at the dark clouds gathering overhead. "Well, if Tom and Walter are willing to go with me, we might be able to get back before it gets too bad."

"I think the hardest job out of all of this was cutting the bastards up. If you want to just go drop them off quickly, that should be easy. I could go with him and leave Tom and Walter here for the leader," Danny suggested.

"Danny, language. You are representing God and that kind of language is not pleasing to Him," Azril scolded.

"You're right, exalted leader. My apology," Danny acknowledged.

"Cory, do you think that Danny would be enough help for you, or would you prefer to have assistance from the other disciples guard?" Azril asked.

"I think the two of us would be enough. As a matter of fact, if you want to join us so you are involved in this process as well, I would feel better about that. Your instruction would be helpful as to where to drop the bags," Cory requested.

Omegra walked up to interject. "I think that is a better idea. Azril, you go with Cory and Danny. You can leave Tom, Walter and Martin here with me. If you would feel more comfortable, we can keep Sara, Debora, Katie and Sharon here as well and I will make sure there is space in the shelter for everyone to be comfortable for the night."

"Perfect," Azril began, as rain started sprinkling from the sky. "We will do one walk around the perimeter to make sure everyone else has left, before we go. Y'all head inside," Azril said, gently kissing his connected partner.

Cory, Danny and Azril walked around within the wall of the City of Disciples to make sure that everyone had gone to seek shelter. Once they were satisfied that no one else was around, the three of them headed out to Cory's vehicle. Cory opened up the back to show the leader the garbage they were going to dispose of. Azril nodded his head, before Cory closed the hatch.

Once the three of them were seated inside the vehicle, Cory started the engine. "Where are we taking this?"

"We can drop it off as far into the new property as possible, then deal with it when we move. If there is an area where there is a line of trees, that would be the best place. That way it will be hidden before we have to deal with it," Azril suggested.

Danny leaned forward from the back seat. "There are a ton of places where we could hide it. The entire fence line of the property is lined with trees in order to maintain privacy from the neighbors. We would just need to make sure to leave a mark somewhere to remind ourselves where it is."

"We can drop the bags off tonight, then immediately head over there and take care of it tomorrow after the purchase is complete," Cory mentioned.

"Perfect, let's go," Azril said, as Cory shifted the vehicle into drive.

By the time they had arrived on the property, it was almost midnight. They were lucky that it was so dark, but that would also give them away if another car just so happened to pass by, so Cory turned off his headlights and backed onto the property as far as he could.

They hoped that they were hidden enough that no one could see them. The three of them exited the vehicle and walked around to the back. Cory opened the hatch and Azril pulled out one of the large garbage bags that contained body parts, as Danny grabbed the other. The bags seemed heavier than they were when they had been placed into the vehicle, so they were being dragged along the ground.

Cory had found a couple of flashlights in the back of his SUV. He handed one to Danny and kept one for himself. They lit their path to the trees and dropped the bags at the base of a large oak, covering them with fallen branches, in order to not only conceal them, but also to mark where they were. As they headed back to their transportation, they heard another vehicle approaching.

"Damn, turn off the flashlights," Azril said, as Cory and Danny grabbed the end of the light, in order to block the illumination.

The three of them froze in place and held their breath, as the approaching vehicle passed by and continued down the road. They all sighed in relief and quickly jumped back into Cory's large SUV.

Danny was shaking and slapping the side of the driver's seat. "Let's get out of here before we get caught."

"Don't wuss out Danny," Cory stated.

"I'm not wussing out. This will be a lot easier once we build the city out here," Danny confessed.

"That's true. Ten foot brick wall all the way around the property, with an enormous wooden gate," Azril admitted.

As Cory drove back to the City of Disciples, the rain had picked up and the windshield wipers were on the highest speed. Cory was leaning over the steering wheel trying to get a better view of the road and Danny was rocking back and forth in his seat, behind Azril.

Sixteen

They were able to make it back to the City of Disciples safely and ran toward the shelter after they exited the vehicle. Tom and Katie were curled up next to each other on the floor to the right of the opening. Walter and Sharon were curled up next to each other on the floor to the left of the opening. Sara, Debora, Martin and Omegra were sitting on the rug in the position that Azril takes when meditating in communication with God.

Azril stood at the edge of the rug, dripping from the rain. "What's going on here?"

Omegra craned her neck to look up at her connected partner. "We were trying to communicate with God. Basically, we were just praying, asking God to keep us safe from the storm."

Azril offered his hand to assist Omegra up off the rug, as the others stood up. "Sounds good. How about we all join in with the evening prayer, then hunker down for the night."

Everyone knelt down where they were and recited the prayer in unison. "At the end of this day, I thank you for all the guidance I have received from you. I hope I have made choices pleasing to you. I have listened to the leader you have chosen for me and can only do what is best for me. Please protect me through this night as I dream of your Promised Land. I am a Disciple of God and I will appease You in worship."

Tom and Katie went back to the position they were in when the leader and head disciples guard entered the shelter, as well as Walter and Sharon. Azril and Omegra took their places on the foam mattress. Martin laid down on the rug, right up against the side of the mattress, flat on his back. Cory and Debora laid down on the rug next to Martin and Danny and Sara laid down on the floor next to Cory and Debora.

The next morning, Beatrice was standing in the opening of the shelter and yelling for the leader before anyone was even awake. "Leader! Leader! Wake up!"

Azril opened his eyes, just as she stepped inside the shelter. Beatrice stepped over the disciples and disciples guard laying on the floor and up to the bed.

"Azril, you're not going to believe this," Beatrice said, excitedly.

Omegra took a deep breath and let it out hard, as she opened her eyes and channeled her sarcasm. "Beatrice, how lovely to see you. What happened?"

"There are new disciples waiting for you outside. Five of them are carrying duffle bags full of money!" Beatrice exclaimed.

Cory and Danny popped up onto their feet and stepped out of the shelter, leaving the others to fully wake up. When the opening of the shelter was parted, Azril peeped through and saw a large crowd gathered in the City of Disciples.

Omegra yawned, propping herself up onto her elbows. "Damn, that's a shit ton of new disciples out there."

"Omegra, darling," Azril scolded, as she laid back down.

"I know," she said, looking up at him, as he hovered his upper body over her.

Omegra draped her right arm over his shoulders and pulled him in for a kiss. They knew Beatrice was still standing next to the bed, but chose to ignore her and continued the embrace. Beatrice began to clear her throat, loudly.

"Did you need something else?" Sara asked Beatrice, as she wedged her way between the inappropriate disciple and the leader.

"That's none of your business," Beatrice told her, taking a couple of steps back.

Luckily, everyone who had slept on the floor was already on their feet. Katie and Tom had stepped out of the shelter with Walter, leaving Sharon behind.

Sharon hooked her hand to her friend's upper arm. "Bea, come on. It's a little crowded in here. Let's go outside."

"Fine. They don't look like they are going to stop any time soon anyway," Beatrice said, referring to the fact that the leader and his connected partner were making out at that point.

Sharon led Beatrice out of the shelter, with Sara, Debora and Martin close behind. Azril and Omegra decided to stay behind, as they chose to engage in connected partner activities.

Cory and Danny led the disciples to the vehicle

where they could open the hatch and shield them from the dripping trees. The rain, as it continued through the night, had cleared up, but the storm left behind a slight breeze. Every time the wind blew over it shook the trees, releasing water droplets down over where they stood.

After opening the hatch to the back of his vehicle, Cory climbed up inside and sat down. Danny produced a small, top flip, spiral notepad and wrote down the names of each disciple who was relinquishing their funds to the City of Disciples. Walter and Tom stood guard outside the shelter, waiting for the leader and his connected partner to emerge, as the head disciples guard counted the funds inside the back of Cory's SUV.

Once he had satisfied his connected partner, Azril approached his head disciples guard, still organizing the funds. "How much did they give you?"

Cory hopped out of the back of his vehicle, then zipped up the duffle bags. "Danny kept track of each disciple's name and the amount they relinquished as I counted it. I counted just under three quarters of a million."

"The amount they told me added up to slightly *over* three quarters of a million. There is enough to pay cash for the property and get started with establishing the city," Danny informed Azril, placing several very full, very heavy duffle bags down on the ledge of the back of the vehicle where Cory was sitting and backed away.

"Sounds like you need to count it again, just to confirm. Does that amount include the quarter of a million we already have?" Azril asked.

Cory unzipped the duffle bags and began re-counting. "No, that's in addition to. Which means we have already had a million dollars relinquished for the City of Disciples."

"Who are the disciples who brought their funds today? I would like to extend my gratitude to them," Azril said.

Danny looked down at the list he had written on his notepad. "Well, with no surprise, Cora and Emma were a couple along with Cora's friend Victoria. Then there was Ruth, who was a young disciple you met recently. Then, there were several who I think would make perfect disciples guard."

"I would like to meet with those who contributed to the City of Disciples after we get back from purchasing the new property. Let's head back to the shelter, so I can give the rundown of what we are going to be doing today to the other disciples guard and Omegra," Azril told them.

Cory finished recounting and confirmed Danny's math, as he climbed out of the back of his SUV and closed the hatch, leaving the duffle bags locked inside. The head disciples guard and the leader headed back toward the shelter where everyone was gathered. Omegra and Martin were standing near the opening of the shelter with Tom and Walter. Sara and Debora were standing off to the side with Sharon and Beatrice.

Azril took the list of new contributors from Danny and handed it to his connected partner. "Hey Martin, I need you to stay with Omegra and the both of you can arrange the meeting with the generous disciples who relinquished their funds this morning. Omegra, make sure everyone who has vowed their loyalty to the City of Disciples receives a uniform. Cory, Danny and I are going to purchase the property and gain access, so we can begin preparing to move the disciples in. I want to make sure that after Omegra and I have our living quarters on the property, my disciples guard is taken care of, then the contributing disciples. Also, I need to know if Emma can make the dark blue uniforms for the disciples after God's cleanse."

Beatrice stomped her foot. "What about me? When do I get my uniform?"

The leader's connected partner snickered. "When you start acting like a disciple."

Beatrice opened her mouth in shock, while Omegra and Martin walked around greeting all of the disciples. Cory and Danny, along with Azril, headed back out to the SUV. The three of them were dressed in their Disciples of God uniforms and ready to make a deal for the large property.

Azril turned his head to look at Cory in the driver's seat to his left. "I know you said that the seller was only looking to recoup the amount they spent on the property, but have you possibly looked it up to know what that amount is?"

"I'm not sure on the exact amount, but it's the price he paid twenty years ago. So it could be about half of what it is actually worth," Cory responded, as he drove toward the brokers office.

Azril had been on his own for so long, he wouldn't even know how to figure out how much a property would cost. He knew about inflation and cost of living prices because his father would always complain about the rise in prices of the farming goods when he was growing up.

Cory parked the vehicle, then turned to look at the leader. "I requested to meet the seller at their brokers office, so they wouldn't find the garbage we placed on the property."

Danny leaned up between the seats. "That was because he made the offer to meet on the property."

"That's perfect. Good thinking," Azril praised Cory.

"Where is the bag of money that we already had before today?" Danny asked.

Azril looked at Danny, as he placed his hand on the door release. "I have it hidden in the shelter at the City of Disciples."

"What if it's needed? Shouldn't you have brought it with you?" Danny wanted to know.

"That is none of your business. Why would you ask a question like that to your leader?" Cory scolded.

"I'm sorry, Leader. Please disregard my inappropriate behavior," Danny apologized.

"Don't worry about it. I can understand the curiosity. Don't be so hard on Danny, Cory. I can see the look of curiosity on your face as well. The difference is, Danny said it out loud and you kept it to yourself. Everyone is different and what is the message I am always preaching about?" Azril asked.

"Tolerance, equality and acceptance," Cory recited.

"That's right. In order to practice tolerance, equality and acceptance, you must be able to understand that everyone is different and not be quick to judge," Azril told Cory.

"I apologize, great leader," Cory said, calmly and with understanding.

Azril placed his left hand on Cory's right arm

that was resting on the center console. "And Danny?"

"Danny, I'm sorry for my judgment and being quick to anger. I didn't mean any malicious intent and I promise it won't happen again," Cory apologized to Danny.

Danny reached up and placed his hand on Cory's shoulder. "I forgive you Cory. God teaches forgiveness, as the leader has supplied the tools for us to follow God's teachings. We are all family and forgiveness is the foundation to a strong family bond."

"I am so proud to have chosen the two of you to be my head disciples guard. This interaction has proven that I could not have chosen two better disciples for that position," Azril praised them, before he opened the passenger side door.

The three of them exited the vehicle and headed inside. There was one person sitting behind a desk, just inside the door, who greeted them. Shortly after that, they were approached by the broker.

"Azril Zion?" the broker asked.

"Yes, that is me," Azril concurred.

"Right this way." The broker led them in a private room near the back of the building. "The seller is already here and has already begun signing the papers to transfer the property to you."

"Thank you. I would like this to go as quickly as possible, so that my guards and I can get started with preparing the property," the leader said.

"Did you bring money?" the seller blurted, as Azril sat down across the table from them.

"I brought cash," Azril said, looking over at Cory, who then rushed out to the vehicle to retrieve the duffle bags. "Although, I haven't been given an exact purchase price."

"Perfect. Sign these papers, then let's complete this transaction. I just want to be rid of the property," the seller commanded.

"Is there a particular reason you are so eager to get rid of the property?" the leader wondered, beginning to look over the paperwork.

The seller poked the table loudly, with his thick finger between sentences. "I'm paying property taxes on twenty thousand acres that I don't even use. People dump trash on that property constantly because they know I'm hardly ever out there and the smell becomes overwhelming. I'm just done trying to keep that dumping ground clear of garbage because the neighbors complain that sometimes what is dumped smells like rotting food, or a dead body. There are too many wild animals out there that tear open trash bags and string the garbage out all over the property. I'm just done with it."

"I can understand that. Have you ever thought of doing something with that property? It's a gorgeous piece of land with lots of potential," Azril inquired.

The seller tapped the papers in front of Azril with his fingertips. "This is my plan right here. I'm seventy four years old and I'm done with it. I drove by last night and I saw someone was out there on the property dumping something. I didn't stop because I knew we were doing this today and figured it was no longer my problem. Good luck with that."

As Azril began signing the papers, Cory re-entered the room and Danny huddled in a corner with him counting out the sale amount. The leader was quietly ecstatic about the fact that they were only having to dish out one hundred thousand for the property. Immediately after passing the cash to the seller, the leader started imagining everything he could do to create the City of Disciples appealing enough to convert outsiders.

Seventeen

Cory collected the ownership paperwork before they headed out of the broker's office, on their way to the property. There was still the matter of hiding the garbage they had dumped the night before.

"Did you remember the shovels?" Azril asked Cory, as they drove to the new property.

"Yes I did. There are three shovels in the

back," Cory told the leader.

"Good. Now we need to figure out where we are going to place the home and the isolation chamber, so we don't accidentally dig the bodies back up during the building process," he told the head disciples guard.

"We could just bury the pieces in one place, then during the building process, move it and bury it forever," Danny suggested.

"I'm sure I know what you are thinking, but I only want to bury it one time and never think about it again," Azril told Danny.

"What about burying it ten feet down in the center of the property?" Cory suggested.

Azril shook his head. "Ten feet should be deep enough, but not in the center. That's where I wanted to build the disciples medical center."

"We could burn the bodies as best we could, then bury it, so it would basically decay into soil," Danny proposed.

Cory looked up at Danny's reflection in the rearview mirror. "That could work, but wouldn't the smell of a burning body disrupt the neighbors like the seller had complained about?"

Azril agreed with Cory. "I think you're right. We need to do something to be sure that there isn't a strong smell. We don't want to draw attention to ourselves."

Cory pulled onto the property and drove back to where the bodies were dropped. "I have an idea. If we bury the body parts and the bags they are in separately, the bodies should eventually moisten and become soil. The bones will become brittle over time and possibly fossilize, but the skin will just decay off the bones."

Azril exited the vehicle and joined the disciples guard around the back to retrieve a shovel. "Look, let's just dig the pit, then throw the body parts in and we can figure out a more permanent disposal method later."

They each pulled out a shovel and headed into the trees. The three of them stopped dead in their tracks when they noticed the spot where they had hidden the body parts the night before, was empty. The garbage bags had been picked up and there wasn't anything to hide. The three of them rushed back to the front of Cory's SUV.

Danny was pacing back and forth, panicking. "Someone found the body parts and has already taken them somewhere else. What do we do?"

"Look, the police aren't here and we didn't own the property when the pieces were found, so let's just put the shovels away and figure out the best placement for the disciples center and housing," Azril told them.

"What if the police connect the bodies to us?"

Danny asked.

Azril walked around to the back of the vehicle and replaced the shovels, before closing the hatch and meandering to the far fence line. "Then we will deal with it when that time comes, but until then, let's just forget about it. Now, I was thinking about placing the house in the back of the property, so we could add the medical center and have room for the crops, flocks and herds. I need two cows and one bull for procreation of the herd in order to have meat along with several chickens and one rooster. With those animals, we have several options of food within the property and the crops will be able to accompany that."

Danny furrowed his brow. "Don't we already have all the crops with the two cows, one bull and a flock of chickens?"

Azril placed his hand on Danny's shoulder. "Yes we do. However, we need to find someone to assist us with moving them from the temporary property to the permanent property."

Cory ignored the problem at hand and joined in the vision of the City of Disciples. "I think we can do that. As for the isolation chamber, what if we buried four shipping containers under the main house. Three we could use for stockpiling supplies and the fourth we could use for isolation."

"I like that idea, but let's do five shipping containers. Three for the supply stockpile and two for the isolation chambers. See how much the shipping containers would be. Also, I'm going to need a hatch from the main house, to get down into the supply and isolation wings," Azril mentioned.

"We could bury one directly below your housing quarters with a private hatch for isolation, then a separate hatch for the supply stockpile. That way, any disciple that needs to go down for supplies won't see the isolation chamber," Cory mentioned.

"I agree. Danny, what do you think?" Azril asked.

"Yes," was all Danny replied, looking around as though there was expectation of a police swarm.

"Let's get back to the City of Disciples before Danny draws too much attention to us," Azril said, heading back toward Cory's vehicle.

Danny sat in the middle of the back seat, looking down nervously, intertwining his fingers. Cory seemed confident and relaxed since the bodies had disappeared.

Eighteen

As they arrived back to the City of Disciples, Omegra and Martin were standing outside the shelter, surrounded by disciples. Azril walked up next to Omegra and saw that the disciples were handing over envelopes and backpacks full of money.

Azril looked out at the new disciples. "My generous, gracious disciples. To those of you who have sold all of your belongings in order to fund the City of Disciples, God has guided me on the path to the property of where the city is to be located. Please inform my partner if you are in need of accommodations. I will be heading out today for temporary tents to place out onto the property in order to begin preparing for the permanent residence for all disciples."

The leader stepped inside the shelter, followed by his head disciples guard. Cory and Danny stood just inside the opening, as Azril gathered the rest of the money that was hidden in the shelter. The disciples guard assisted the leader with removing all of Azril's belongings and disassembling the shelter.

The leader emerged from the shelter. "To all the disciples here, we are going to need assistance with transporting the crops along with the few animals we have. Would anyone like to volunteer to assist with that?"

Sara raised her hand. "I can take some of the crops and the chickens, but we might want to get some planting pots in order to safely transport the crops. I would be afraid that if we just dug them up and then tried to replant them on the new property, they may not survive."

Azril pointed at her in acknowledgment. "We can accommodate that. Cory, take Tom and Walter up to the hardware store and purchase some planting pots. Bring them back here for the disciples to transfer the crops from the ground."

"What about the disciples that need temporary housing?" Danny asked.

"When Cory gets back, the three of us will be heading out to the sporting goods store in order to purchase the tents. Omegra, Would you like to go with us?" Azril informed.

Omegra hooked her arm around his waist. "I would love to join you, but as your connected partner, I feel as though it would be more beneficial for me to stay in the City of Disciples with Martin."

Azril kissed his connected partner on her temple. "You're right. At least one of us should be in the City of Disciples at all times."

"I'll go with you, Leader," Beatrice said, emphatically.

"As a matter of fact, once we get to the permanent property, you will be placed in a temporary isolation chamber," the leader informed the disciple.

"This isn't fair! I'm suppose to be your companion and I should be exempt from being placed in isolation!" Beatrice screamed and stomped her foot.

"Martin and Danny, can you please help me

take down the wooden frame of the shelter, so we can use most of this for the temporary isolation," Azril instructed, ignoring Beatrice.

"You can't just ignore me. We are companions and I should be treated the same as your connected partner," Beatrice complained.

Omegra rolled her eyes. "At most, you are a disciple. At the least, you are a follower staying in the City of Disciples."

"This is…" Beatrice began.

"Hey Bea, why don't you come over here with me," Sharon interrupted.

"Thank you, Sharon," Azril said, as she led Beatrice away.

Martin and Danny had pulled down the canvas tarp from the shelter and began disassembling the wooden frame. Sara and Debora were folding the meditation carpet and tarp, as Azril and Omegra organized all the items that were inside the shelter.

Buddy had been wandering off the property more and more, along with staying away for longer periods of time. As Cory, Tom and Walter returned with the planting pots, Buddy returned, followed by another dog and five puppies. Buddy was a German shepherd, but the other dog was a golden retriever. The mixed puppies were adorable and Omegra swooned over the babies.

Omegra sat down on the ground and encouraged the puppies to approach her. "Oh Buddy, now we know why you have been gone for a couple of days."

Azril pet his companion on the top of his head. "Buddy, did you get yourself your own connected partner?"

Buddy barked in response and the golden retriever sat next to Omegra, as the puppies fought for a place in her lap. Sara and Debora joined the leader's connected partner on the ground, so they could also interact with the puppies.

"Can we take them to the new City of Disciples with us?" Omegra asked.

"Only if they want to come with us. Buddy has always been a free agent, to come and go as he pleases," Azril explained.

"You want to come with us, don't you Buddy?" Omegra said. "How about you, Lady?"

"Is that what we are calling her now, Lady?" Azril asked.

"Why not? We can have Buddy and Lady, then we can name the puppies once we learn their personalities," Omegra suggested.

"Cory, you don't mind transporting the dogs to the new City of Disciples, do you?" Azril asked.

"I don't mind at all, Leader," Cory responded.

"Great, let's pack up some things and start

taking it over to the new property," Azril suggested.

Omegra and Sara each picked up two puppies and stood, as Debora grabbed puppy number five and joined them on her feet. Lady stayed close by Omegra, while Buddy stayed close to Azril. They all headed toward Cory's SUV. Danny opened the hatch for Buddy and Lady to jump up inside, then the disciples and the leader's connected partner placed the puppies inside with the two other dogs.

"Cory, take us over to the new City of Disciples. I would like to get Buddy and his family familiar with their new home," Azril told his head disciples guard.

"No problem, Leader," Cory responded.

Cory and Danny climbed into the front seat of Cory's vehicle, as Azril and Omegra climbed into the back seat with Martin. Tom and Walter rode in Tom's car, as the other disciples all packed up the vehicles they had traveled in and followed behind as a caravan to the City of Disciples as well.

"When we arrive to the City of Disciples, Omegra and Martin will stay, while the three of us head out to purchase tents for temporary housing," Azril informed them, as Cory drove toward the property.

"I was thinking that the tents could be used for

temporary housing after the permanent disciple residence is built. The disciples will be assigned a permanent housing assignment and as the outsiders come in, they will need somewhere to stay until they go through God's cleanse and receive their permanent housing assignment," Omegra suggested.

"Sounds perfect. That way, the new disciples will already be on the property and within the limits of the City of Disciples. Everyone in a light blue uniform will be housed temporarily in the tents," Azril said.

"Exactly what I was thinking. Since the disciples before God's cleanse can't leave the boundary of the City of Disciples, the tents would be perfect," Omegra agreed.

"It's more for the fact that before God's cleanse, the new disciples have the option to request to leave," Azril responded.

Danny turned in his seat, to look at the leader behind him. "If they request to leave before God's cleanse, what happens to the funds they relinquished to the City of Disciples? Is that given back?"

"No, it was relinquished to the City of Disciples. The only monetary funds they will be able to leave the City of Disciples with, is what they were compensated for while working in the City of Disciples," Azril told him.

Cory pulled up to the property and parked his vehicle. They all waited for the disciples to park their vehicles as well, before exiting. Once everyone was gathered around Cory's vehicle, Azril opened the hatch to let the dogs out. Buddy and Lady sat next to the leader and his connected partner, as the puppies were set down on the ground to sniff around and get acquainted with their new surroundings.

"To the disciples that have crops and animals in their vehicles, see Omegra for proper placement," Azril began. "The housing area will be along the back of the property line, as far away from the front of the property as possible. That is to ensure the safety of the disciples. There will be a medical center built directly in the middle of the property. I am leaving with the head disciples guard to purchase temporary housing tents for everyone to stay in."

As the leader, with Cory and Danny returned to the vehicle, the disciples immediately began unpacking the City of Disciples resources. Azril counted out twenty thousand dollars from the duffle bag that was sitting at his feet. He felt as though that was enough for everything they would need for all the items they were going to purchase.

It wasn't long before Cory pulled into the parking lot of the sporting goods store. He drove around the parking lot trying to choose a space that was close to the doors, due to the large purchase they were about to make. After exiting the vehicle, the three of them headed up to the doors.

"I'm thinking about several different sizes of tents. For me and Omegra, I will need one with two separate rooms, as well as a sunroom. The others need to be large enough to live in, not just the small sleeping areas," Azril explained, as they arrived at the camping area.

"How many disciples are now living in the City of Disciples?" Cory asked.

"I'm thinking that we can get five hundred tents, plus the one for me and Omegra," Azril answered.

They emptied out the entire aisle of tents. It was only two of five different sizes. The leader wanted temporary housing for at least two thousand disciples until they were able to complete the disciple's resident building. Some of the tents were single rooms, where others were multiple rooms.

Cory found an employee walking by. "Excuse me? Do you happen to have any more of these tents in your warehouse area?"

"We may have a few more of each size. How

many are you needing?" the sales associate asked.

Azril stepped up next to Cory. "We have ten here. Do you happen to have ninety more back there?"

"Let me check to see what we have here. We can always order the rest and have them delivered to you," the sales associate suggested.

"Are you able to have them delivered today?" Azril asked.

"If they are in stock at the stores within fifty miles of the delivery area, yes they can be delivered today. If not, the rest would be delivered tomorrow," the sales associate informed him.

Azril nodded and the employee headed to the back receiving area. When he reemerged, he had four more of each of the five sizes. That gave them thirty tents.

"This leaves you with needing seventy more. Let's go over to the customer service area and I will get those tents on order for you," the sales associate told them.

They were lucky enough to have the rest of the tents they needed at seven stores close enough to the property. They placed the order, then headed over to the register to pay for the tents they were able to purchase from that location.

When they checked out, they were purchasing

not only the tents, but also cots, sleeping bags and chairs. Several sales associates assisted them out to the vehicle to help pack what they could in the back. What wouldn't fit, Azril chose to purchase a small tow trailer and tied the rest down on the trailer.

Once they were ready to go, they headed back to the City of Disciples for set up. By the time they had arrived, the contributing disciples were preparing a section of the property to set up the tents, as well as preparing the crops for planting.

Azril requested the disciples to gather around him. "My loyal disciples. I appreciate the contribution and assistance with preparing the City of Disciples. I have purchased temporary housing tents for us all to stay within the confines of the city. Some we were able to bring with us, whereas others will be delivered soon. Once we have the tents setup, I would like to meet with each of you individually, in order to assign work detail. Please refer to your Disciples Doctrine in order to understand your place within the City of Disciples."

Nineteen

T he disciples assisted with unpacking the items from the trailer, as well as the back of Cory's vehicle. They were also working to set up the tents in a large circle with enough room between each, in order to be inviting. The large open area in the middle was to be set up as the worship area.

Once Azril and Omegra had set up their own

housing tent, the leader stood in the sunroom area. "If you have finished setting up the tents, please have a seat in the worship area and I will call you in from the list I was supplied with. I will be assigning housing for the ones on the list and preaching to any extra disciples that have joined us. If you don't receive a shelter assignment, that means that you haven't contributed to the City of Disciples and you will need to familiarize yourself with the Disciples Doctrine."

Cory and Danny stood outside the tent opening, with Omegra slightly behind Azril to his right and Martin to his left. Omegra placed her hand, lovingly, on the leader's shoulder.

Azril reached up and touched his connected partner's hand, turning toward the disciples guard on his other side. "Martin, before I start with anyone out there, I would like to just let you know, your housing tent will be right next to ours. As a matter of fact, I will have you staying in the tent with Cory and Danny. I need the three of you as close to us as possible without actually being in this tent with us."

Martin leaned slightly closer to the leader, speaking quietly. "Is it possible to get a single sleeping tent for me? I've had top surgery, but not bottom surgery and there are times I still have a fear that I could be taken advantage of. I'm not saying that Cory, or Danny would do anything to harm me, but I would just feel more comfortable if I was able to have my own private sleeping quarters."

"I'm sure we can accommodate that. I want to make sure all of the disciples in the City of Disciples are comfortable and if that is what makes you comfortable, I will make that happen. Thank you, Martin for trusting me as your leader to be vulnerable with me," Azril reassured him, before turning to his connected partner. "Omegra, please let Cory know I will need to see him first, then Danny."

Omegra nodded and poked her head out of the opening of the tent, tapping Cory on the shoulder. He turned and entered the tent.

Cory stood at attention in front of Azril. "What can I do for you?"

"I need the disciples guard to move the tents around just a bit," the leader began. "This will be something that will need to be understood by the disciples. I know they worked hard to set up the living quarters, but remember there are more that are going to be delivered. I need you and Danny in the same tent and Martin has requested a single private tent. I have granted his request and would like the tent that you and Danny choose to be basically attached to the tent Martin will choose. So, you and Danny can get a two room tent and the single room tent that Martin wants, then tie the securing poles together as if Martin is just living in a detached room. That will need to be placed right next to the leader tent."

"No problem, leader. I will take care of that. Now, some of the disciples wanted to ask about their vehicles. Did you want them to sell their vehicles for the funds, or keep them for transportation?" Cory wondered.

Azril shook his head aggressively. "No, only your vehicle is for disciple transportation, in order to recruit new disciples. If we have to, we can take all of the other disciple's vehicles to trade in for a large van that could fit ten disciples in the back, on top of the driver and passenger. Other than that, none of the disciples need to have their vehicles. That is a potential for defection."

"I could also contribute to the trade in as well with my SUV," Cory informed him.

"I appreciate the offer Cory, but we need your vehicle for small errands, whereas the large van will be specific to transporting disciples with the intention of recruiting outsiders. Please let Danny know I will need to see him before I start to talk with the disciples," the leader told Cory.

Cory nodded before he stepped out and let Danny know his presence was being requested.

Danny stepped inside the tent and stood in front of the leader.

Azril repeated his request to the other head disciples guard. "Danny, I have already addressed this with Martin and Cory, but you and Cory will be assigned to the same tent. Martin will be in a single tent attached to the two room tent for you and Cory. I will need the three of you to remain as close to me, as the leader and my connected partner, as possible."

Danny produced a thick envelope from his pocket and held it out for the leader. "I can agree with that. I actually have an envelope of funds for the City of Disciples as well. All of my belongings sold and I decided that none of it was important to me, as it was just a reminder of a previous life."

"Why didn't you give this to me sooner?" Azril wanted to know, passing the envelope to Omegra.

"I had a couple of items that still needed to be paid for before I gave it to you," Danny admitted.

"That's very admirable, Danny. I really appreciate your loyalty and dedication to the Disciples of God," Azril told him.

Danny knelt down in front of Azril. "You are the leader of the disciples. I trust you as my leader. As the leader of the Disciples of God, I pledge my loyalty to not only you, but also to God."

"Azril, I need to speak to you," Beatrice yelled

from outside of the tent.

Danny darted out of the tent, after he had received his blessing, to assess the situation before Azril had to deal with it. The leader hugged his connected partner before preparing himself to see what was going on.

"Martin, stay here with Omegra. I need to deal with this," Azril said, kissing his connected partner, then headed out of the tent. "Beatrice, calm down. I just don't understand why I can't seem to complete any leader tasks without you being disruptive. What is your problem now?"

"Tom and Walter are constructing a small frame for what I was told was to be the isolation cage for me. First of all, it's not even big enough for me to stand up in and second, why is it being made for *me*?" Beatrice said, irate.

"It's being erected for isolation, yes. It's not just for *you*. You will, however, be the first to be placed in it if you can't control yourself," the leader informed.

"Why am I the only disciple being forced into isolation?" Beatrice whined.

"At this point, you are the only disciple committing evil acts. You need time to familiarize yourself with the Disciples Doctrine and I think that you would also benefit from some one on one worship services," Azril told her.

"How long will I have to be in isolation?" Beatrice inquired.

"Omegra believes that seven days for your first official time in isolation should be adequate," Azril explained.

Beatrice rolled her eyes and pursed her lips. "Why is Omegra deciding on how much time I'm spending in isolation? That should be your choice."

"Other than being disruptive and inappropriate with me, you are committing more evil acts against Omegra. Also, she is my connected partner and she has the same authority as I do," the leader told her.

Beatrice took a step closer to the leader, but Cory held her back. "I think you are allowing Omegra to undermine you with the disciples and maybe you should ask her to give you your balls back, so you can sack up and lead the disciples your way and not the way your woman is telling you to."

Azril was done listening to her. "You are now not only being disrespectful to me and God, but now you are being disrespectful to the disciples. Cory, please remove the disciple from the option of getting a housing assignment. She needs to be held near the isolation area until it is completed and she can start her time."

The leader turned and headed back into his tent with his connected partner and Martin. They could hear Beatrice screeching, as Cory dragged her to the back of the property where Tom and Walter were putting together the isolation chamber. Danny gave Azril a few moments to regroup before sending in the disciples for their housing assignments.

Azril was happy to see Sara was the first disciple sent in. "I am so sorry you had to witness the disrespect from a fellow disciple. Thank you so much for your patience with the situation. Now Sara, I'm thinking you and Debora could be roommates in a two room tent. That would mean that the two of you are in one of the rooms and there would be two other disciples on the other side, in the other room. That is only if you are comfortable with that."

"I'm okay with that, as long as Beatrice isn't in the other room," Sara said, biting her thumbnail.

"Not at all. I have a special assignment for her. Anyway, please ask Debora, Katie and Sharon to join you in here," Azril informed.

"That would be amazing to have them in the same tent with me. Yay," Sara said, bouncing on her toes, then popping her head out of the tent.

She called in the other three disciples and they joined everyone inside the sunroom area of the leader tent. Each one of them were creating high pitched squeals in excitement after being informed of the assignment.

"Can we also get a tent next to the disciples guard? Katie requested.

"I know what you are thinking. Here is the deal, Cory, Danny and Martin are going to be in two separate tents on one side here, with Tom and Walter on the other side. There will be tents next to those with other disciples guard in them once they have been selected. There will be at least two tents between yours and theirs, depending upon what side you pick will depend upon which two you are closest to. Just make sure that you are aware of the message in the Disciples Doctrine," Azril told them.

The four disciples giggled and left, happy with their assignment. Since Emma was the official disciple uniform seamstress, the leader wanted to keep her close by. She was assigned a single room tent next to Sara, Debora, Katie and Sharon. The rest of the disciples were assigned randomly and luckily the rest of the tents had been delivered just as he had finished with all of the assignments.

Twenty

The disciples who had contributed to the funding of the City of Disciples were the only ones who were assigned a housing arrangement within the circle with the leader and his connected partner. Omegra and Azril began setting up their tent, while the other disciples prepared their shelters. The leader's housing was larger than any of the disciples shelters.

Azril was setting up the sunroom area as his meeting space with the disciples and disciples guard. Further into the tent, the leader was using the center as his meditation area and he had placed the meditation carpet there. The room to the left of that, was the room that he and Omegra shared for their connected partner activities and sleep. The room to the right of the meditation area, the leader used as an office. Omegra would be using the office more, as she would be the one to organize the finances.

Tom stepped up to the outside of Azril's tent and called out for him. "Leader, we would like for you to examine the isolation chamber we have built."

The leader emerged from his sunroom. Walter had joined Tom and they were standing there, smiling as if they were proud of themselves.

"Has Beatrice been contained?" Azril asked.

Walter hooked his hands behind his back and rocked back and forth on his feet, "Yes. Once we had constructed the frame, we put her inside to finish with the design."

"Well, let's go see what you have done," Azril said, motioning for them to lead the way.

As they got closer, they could hear Beatrice yelling from the isolation chamber. "Let me out of here! This isn't fair! I'm going to be the leader's connected partner! You can't do this to me!"

Azril walked around the isolation, ignoring her, realizing that it was more like a human cage. "How are we suppose to get her out when her time is up?"

The isolation chamber had been built as a box that was basically two feet wide by three feet tall. There were wooden bars, about five inches apart, all the way around the sides and along the top with a flat piece of plywood on the bottom. Beatrice was sitting in the cage, grasping onto two of the wooden bars, yelling through the space between them.

"Oh good, Azril help me," Beatrice pleaded.

Azril continued ignoring the disciple and only addressed his disciples guard. "Don't we need some kind of door to open in order for her, or anyone else to get in and out?"

"It's on top," Tom responded, showing the leader the hinges and lock on the top portion of the cage.

"Okay. So tell me about your thought process with the design," Azril inquired.

"It's more of a deterrent. No one wants to be placed in isolation if they know they can't stand up for the time they are going to be locked up," Walter told him.

"I get it, but this seems a little inhumane," Azril

told them.

"Exactly, now get me out of here," Beatrice complained.

"So for the next isolation chamber, make sure it is big enough for them to move around a little more," Azril mentioned.

"The next one? You mean I have to stay in this cage for seven days like this?" Beatrice asked.

Azril crouched down next to the cage and glared at the disciple. "Beatrice, you have placed not only me in an uncomfortable situation, but also my connected partner, as well as the other disciples. Maybe if you are uncomfortable for a few days, you will understand."

Beatrice screamed, as the leader and the disciples guard walked away, back toward the housing area. "You can't leave me like this!"

"Thank goodness you built it far enough away that her screams are only a distant buzz from the main area," Azril said.

"Tom locked me in it before we locked her in, just to make sure that it would keep her contained without needing a constant guard," Walter mentioned.

"Sounds to me that you two were having a good time constructing something for use. How do you feel about being in charge of the team of disciples who will be building the permanent housing?" Azril asked, as Omegra approached them.

The leader wrapped his arms around her and embraced his connected partner, as Tom and Walter walked away, leaving the two of them alone. Omegra had proved her loyalty to not only the leader, but also to God and proved that she absolutely trusted Azril's judgement. Even with the over affectionate disciple, she allowed him to deal with the isolation without telling him what to do.

"You know that there is a possibility that Beatrice could be shunned from the City of Disciples, right? How do you think the other disciples would feel about that?" Omegra asked, as the leader released her from his embrace.

"I think that would test the loyalty of the disciples. It would be unfortunate if we would have to shun their biological family members, if it came down to that. We know they don't mind the shunning ceremonies, but at this point it has only been outsiders who have caused harm to the disciples," Azril mentioned.

"I will say though, I can't wait until we have some other connected partners here in the City of Disciples," Omegra said.

"I think that Cory and Debora, along with Danny and Sara will come to me soon to schedule their connection ceremonies. I don't know how much longer they can wait before engaging in connected partner activities. I know God would not approve if they were to become one flesh before getting to know each other and know for sure that they would want to be connected partners," Azril told her.

"I believe that Tom and Katie, along with Walter and Sharon are also getting closer," Omegra admitted.

"I'm just glad that Sharon is flourishing in the City of Disciples. I was afraid that after the shunning of Egon, she was going to spiral and want to leave," Azril said.

"Does Beatrice know that Sharon and Walter have been talking? I have heard rumblings that she has been claiming that her and Sharon have offered themselves to you and they are to be treated with the same respect as the disciples show you," Omegra mentioned.

Azril rubbed his forehead and took a deep breath. "Why is it that she seems to think that she is more important than you are? How about you do the private one on one worship sessions with her? I will let you decide when she is ready to get out. For now she has seven days, but if she refuses to respect you, keep her there as long as you deem necessary until she treats you the same as she treats me."

"I absolutely do not want her to obsess over me the way she does you," Omegra said, laughing.

"Cute," Azril said, kissing her.

Omegra and Azril meandered toward their tent in order to engage in connected activities, while the disciples were working around the City of Disciples and being monitored by the disciples guard. Tom and Walter took turns walking back and forth to keep an eye on Beatrice. Cory and Danny kept watch on the disciples tending to the crops and the animals. One of the disciples was able to find an outsider willing to assist with transporting the cow and bull to the City of Disciples with the new calf. The outsider was also receptive to sticking around and hearing the message from the Disciples Doctrine.

Everyone in a light blue uniform had a lawn tool. Some were raking the ground, some were using manual rototillers and others marking trees in order to remove them for the permanent housing building. When Azril and Omegra re-emerged from their shelter, the leader motioned for his head disciples guard to join him in his sunroom.

"Have y'all been able to find the remaining members of the disciples guard?" Azril asked.

Cory stood at attention before speaking. "Actually yes. Danny, Tom, Walter and I have made sure to select those who we thought would be loyal."

"What about Martin? Did you make sure to include him in the selections?" Azril wanted to know.

Danny shrugged his shoulders. "Martin said his focus was Omegra and to make sure she was safe, so he was okay with us selecting the other seven who would be under your instruction."

"Sounds perfect. I'm glad that he is loyal to his job assignment. Could you please gather those that you have chosen over here, so I could meet them?" Azril requested.

Cory headed off to gather those chosen to be in the disciples guard. Martin was the first to arrive, as he always made sure to stay close to Omegra. Tom and Walter were next. They were talking and laughing with one another. Shortly after, Cory and Danny arrived, followed by the rest of the disciples chosen as the disciples guard. Omegra kissed Azril on his cheek, before heading off to mingle with the disciples.

Azril assessed the potential disciples guard before pointing at Cory. "Okay everyone, I would just like to make sure you know each other and you're comfortable interacting with each other. Remember, the message here in the City of Disciples is acceptance, equality and tolerance. Stand up and introduce yourselves to the group along with a short detail as to what drew you to the Disciples of God."

"Hello, I'm Cory. I was in a religious studies class with our great leader, Azril. He challenged the professor and made some great points. I agreed with the leader and followed him out when he was kicked out of the lecture hall."

"Hi, I'm Danny. I walked out with Cory from the same religious studies class. We were taking that class to find purpose in life and we feel as though following Azril as the leader of the Disciples of God is the path we were meant to take."

"I'm Martin. I have just wanted to feel accepted for who I am my entire life. My parents kicked me out when I was fourteen and I was forced to live with my aunt and uncle who loved me for who I was and who I wanted to be. I'm hoping to have them join us here in the City of Disciples."

"Hello, I'm Tom. I have been bullied most of my life. I went to a private christian school and most of those kids were there because their parents didn't want to deal with them. It was similar to a boarding school, except we went home on the weekends. When I would voice my disdain for the school to my parents, they would tell me I was overreacting. I just want to feel cared for."

"I'm Walter. My brothers, Jerry and Lawerence

and I recently lost our parents in a fatal car accident. We were looking for purpose in life when I found Azril and the Disciples of God. After reading through the Disciples Doctrine, I told my brothers about the disciples, they sold everything we owned and we have committed ourselves to the City of Disciples and our great leader, Azril."

Azril held his hands up to welcome the first seven. "We are only half way through the disciples guard and I absolutely appreciate every single one of you. I need every one of you to be sure that you are enforcing disciple law. Let's continue, then we will talk about the first assignment I have for the twelve of you."

"Hello everyone, I'm Sean. I have never been religious and my parents are atheist. I'm just tired of the hate in the world and I was looking into religion thinking it would help me find people who are less likely to spew hate. I was ready to give up, thinking that the world was just full of hateful people, until I heard the leader speak about the Disciples of God. I immediately felt as though I had found a place of love, rather than hate."

"Hey, I'm Joe. My sister Farrah actually forced me to come listen to the leader speak on the college campus. I took her in when she was sixteen and told my parents that she was trans. My sister was born as Adam. My mother told her if she wanted to be gay, they would be okay with that, but they were not okay with her changing everything about herself. My dad told her to man up and started beating on her when she changed her wardrobe.

"When Farrah called me and told me that she was trans, I congratulated her for finally being comfortable enough to come out. She asked if she could come stay with me for a little while and I told her she could. When I saw her and realized my father had beat her, I fought for her to live with me. She was on campus one day and saw the leader preaching on the lawn, purchased a Disciples Doctrine, then forced me to listen to the leader the next day.

"After listening to him speak, I purchased my own copy of the Disciples Doctrine and Farrah and I sold everything we owned to be a part of the Disciples of God. I feel honored that I was chosen to be part of the disciples guard."

"I just heard my roommate Stephen talking about the Disciples of God with his friend David and I just hate the idea of college. I decided to join them here and I have never felt better about my decision. That means I can get away from my overbearing mother. Oh, my name is Warren."

Azril had them all stand in a line, so he could shake their hands and properly welcome them as the twelve disciples guard. "Cory, Danny, Martin, Tom, Walter, Jerry, Lawerence, Sean, Joe, Stephen, David and Warren. Welcome to the City of Disciples. Those of you in the light blue uniform, please go with Cory to meet up with Emma and exchange it for the grey uniform. Cory and Danny are the head disciples guard, so if you have any concerns, please take it to one of them. They will then decide whether they can take care of it, or bring it to me. Martin is Omegra's personal head disciples guard. If at any time you feel that she may be in danger, please let him know. Thank you for your loyalty to the Disciples of God."

Twenty One

Once Cory had returned with the new disciples guard, the leader made sure to assign them housing tents in the area that was cordoned off for the disciples guard. Danny, Tom and Walter were taking turns checking on Beatrice, Martin was keeping an eye on Omegra and the leader was instructing the new guards to keep a watch on the rest of the disciples. Azril decided he was going to watch the new disciples guard to see how loyal they all were to the City of Disciples.

After about an hour, Azril gathered eleven of the disciples guard. "I need three of you to go with Cory to find five shipping containers. The rest of you are going to join Tom and Walter with supervising the disciples as they dig on the property, in order to bury those shipping containers. Three of those containers are going to be used to stockpile supplies within the City of Disciples. The other two are going to be used as isolation chambers. Does everyone understand what the purpose of the isolation chamber is?"

Jerry raised his hand. "In the Disciples Doctrine, it states since the outsiders have cages to hold those who were engaging in evil acts, the disciples will have similar cages for isolation. The isolation chambers are for anyone in the City of Disciples with evil intent. If a disciple goes against God, or the leader, they would be placed in isolation. If an outsider comes in the City of Disciples saying they want to learn about the disciples, when in actuality they are there under false pretenses, they are to be placed in isolation. As such, anyone sent to isolation will be there for a set period of time determined upon the action they committed. In that same context, each disciple in isolation would be required to read God's message as written in the Disciples Doctrine."

"Exactly," Azril agreed.

Jerry continued. "For any outsiders who are inside the City of Disciples that end up in isolation, they are required to participate in personal worship sessions with the leader of the disciples. The leader will determine as to whether or not the one in isolation has become a loyal follower of God as portrayed in the Disciples Doctrine before they are able to be released. Anyone inside the City of Disciples who commits any of the evil acts mentioned in the Disciples Doctrine, will be placed in isolation for a set period of time determined upon the action. Once their time has been completed, the isolated disciple, or outsider must receive one cut from each disciple affected by their actions."

Lawerence decided to continue with the message from the Disciples Doctrine. "With that being said, any disciple, or outsider who is released from isolation and after they receive their cuts, they must agree to live in the City of Disciples. They must also follow God's message as written in the Disciples Doctrine. The leader will share this message with all disciples through the worship service. If they refuse, the leader must then shun them from the physical land, just as God will shun them from the promised land."

Walter, seeming to feel upstaged by his brothers, decided to finish the message. "The isolation chambers are to be used as reflection rooms. Some disciples will spend only a few hours with the leader in personal worship, whereas others will spend a few days reflecting upon their actions along with making the decision to stay in the City of Disciples or risk being shunned not only from the physical land, but also by God in the promised land."

Sean turned toward Azril. "So you want the isolation chambers to basically seem like solitary confinement, is that right?"

The leader placed his hand on Sean's shoulder. "Essentially yes, but they need to be comfortable and invoke peace. We want the disciples to want to stay and understand that this is the only path to get to the promised land with God."

"I know where we can get those shipping containers," Stephen mentioned.

"Thank you, Stephen. I appreciate your initiative. You can take Warren and David with you when you go with Cory," Azril said.

In order to be sure that the disciples guard was held accountable, the leader divided them into tiers. Cory was the head of the first tier with Warren, David and Stephen. Danny was the head of the second tier with Tom, Jerry and Lawerence.

Martin was to be the head of the third tier with Walter, Joe and Sean. Azril wanted to be sure that the chain of command was upheld.

The leader dismissed the disciples guard. Tier one went to pick up the shipping containers while tiers two and three headed out to grab a few disciples to begin digging. Once they were on their way to their job assignments, Azril grabbed his Disciples Doctrine and headed out to interact with the followers who were assisting the disciples with the crops and animals.

"Debora, Sara, it's so great to see you here. I'm so glad that y'all contributed to the City of Disciples," the leader said.

"We are honored to be here, Leader. We also brought our friend Beth who contributed along with her friend Samantha," Sara informed Azril.

"I'm so glad to hear that." The leader placed his hand on each of their foreheads for blessing. "Make sure to get with Omegra, so they can receive their uniforms. I hope to meet all the new disciples that have joined us and contributed to the City of Disciples. We are beginning to flourish and I am hoping to save more people and bring them here into the City of Disciples."

Azril continued to walk around on the property, blessing each disciple he came into contact with. Each and every one of them bowed in front of the leader as he placed his hand on their head. The disciples were working diligently to prepare the property as a permanent living space.

Twenty Two

When tier one of the disciples guard returned, there were five trucks following behind Cory's vehicle. Those trucks were towing the shipping containers that had been requested. Tiers two and three of the disciples guard were still digging in the back of the property with several disciples.

Cory parked and exited his vehicle, before walking back to the truck directly behind him.

"Thank you gentlemen. If you could drop off those shipping containers toward the back of the property. We have some disciples back there digging in order to bury these."

The first driver saluted with two fingers from his left hand and headed to the back of the property. The other drivers followed behind the first. Azril waved as each of the drivers passed by.

David approached the leader. "The drivers are Vernon, Orlean, Paul, Damon and Antonio. They are willing to hear your message. We all spoke to them about the disciples and they seem interested."

Azril gathered all of the tier one disciples guard. "If they join us and contribute to the City of Disciples, you all will be compensated. Each one of you is appreciated."

The leader headed back to his housing tent and allowed his disciples guard, as well as the other disciples, to continue working. He stopped over to check on Omegra before meandering into the sunroom area of his shelter. The leader checked the list of disciples that had already contributed to the City of Disciples, along with each job assignment for them.

He needed to figure out what each disciple would be paid daily, in order to keep things equal, but also to encourage them to continue recruiting outsiders. He sat down and began writing notes for the next sermon.

The new disciples, before God's cleanse, would be paid two dollars per day. God's cleanse would be like a promotion and they would then be paid five dollars per day.

Once they get to level one, they will be paid ten dollars per day with a two dollar, one time, bonus for each outsider they bring in. At level two, they will be paid fifteen dollars per day with the same bonus for the outsiders. At level three, they will be paid twenty dollars per day with the same bonus for the outsiders. At level four, they will be paid twenty five dollars per day with the same bonus for the outsiders.

As for the disciples guard, they will be compensated thirty dollars per day. They have the opportunity to receive the bonus if they go out to recruit outsiders with the disciples. Since Cory is the designated driver in his vehicle for errands, Azril decided that the disciples guard should take turns in the disciple van, taking them out for conversion.

As a stipulation for the disciples to keep an eye on their recruits, there would be a fee if their recruited disciple is shunned. The disciple who recruited them, will then have to pay back the two dollar bonus they received. As for their pay, the disciples will have to pay for their uniforms after receiving their first one.

As the followers arrive into the City of Disciples, they are relinquishing all of their funds from the physical land. They are given one light blue uniform for them to wear. After they participate in God's cleanse, they are then issued one dark blue uniform as they exchange it for the one before. The same goes as they level up. Their first uniform is exchanged for the next. If they would like more than one uniform, they will have to pay for it with their compensation.

It will be recommended that each disciple have at least eight uniforms in order to be able to change daily and have something to wear while their uniforms are being washed. Once the disciples housing building is erected, there would be more job assignments to go around.

The chain of command is stated in the Disciples Doctrine under the Converting Outsiders chapter. If any disciple has any concerns, they would have to move through the ranks up to the head disciples guard, depending upon which tier they were assigned. Each disciple would be assigned to the disciples guard tiers as they are recruited, in order to make things more simple. The head disciples guard will then bring any concerns to the leader. Azril will then either address those concerns with the disciple personally, or give the solution to the disciples guard to relay to the disciple.

Omegra distracted the leader when she entered the tent. "Hey Azril, is there anything I can help you with?"

"Actually, yes. Can you get Cory for me? I have something I need him to do," he told her.

Omegra nodded and skittered off. As Azril waited, he prepared a sermon for the first night in the new City of Disciples. He wanted to be sure the disciples knew what was expected of them from God within the City of Disciples.

Cory entered the tent, with Omegra close behind. "You wanted to see me Leader?"

Azril stood to be face to face with his head disciples guard. "Yes, Cory. I need you to take one other disciple to the store with you. I need envelopes that I can write the disciples names on and place payment in for their disciple work. Also, I need you to get walkie talkies for the disciples guard as well as for both me and Omegra. We will need a total of fourteen. I want to be able to communicate with y'all, at all times. Be sure that they are compatible with each other. On top of that, we are going to need to feed the disciples soon. If y'all could pick up food and water for everyone, please."

"Absolutely, great leader," Cory agreed.

Cory chose to take Debora with him, as Omegra and Azril stayed in the their tent, preparing the sermon.

Twenty Three

Just before Cory and Debora returned, Danny entered the leader's housing tent. Azril wasn't sure what time it was at that point, but he knew the disciples had been working most of the day.

Danny bowed down in front of Azril. "Oh great leader, there have been several disciples requesting sustenance."

The leader invoked a blessing upon his disciples guard. "Of course. They have been working so hard all day. Cory and Debora should be back soon with something for everyone to eat."

Azril picked up his Disciples Doctrine and prepared himself for the sermon that he had decided would take place after everyone was able to eat. He stepped out of the circle of tents and saw some of the disciples had gathered into a group and were no longer working, whereas others were still preparing the crops for the City of Disciples.

Azril announced loudly across the property in order to get the attention of all the disciples as well as the disciples guard. "My loyal disciples, please join me in the worship area. I apologize that I have lost track of time and hope you are willing to forgive me."

Several disciples began gathering the yard tools and others were getting to know each other. The leader greeted each disciple as they stepped between the tents and into the worship area. Each one of them were smiling and accepted the blessing as they passed by the leader of the physical land.

"My loyal disciples," Azril started, once everyone was seated and he was standing in front of them. Even Buddy, Lady and their five puppies came in to join. "Everyone of you has worked so hard today and I really appreciate your dedication to God. I understand you are looking for sustenance and I promise it is on its way. Debora and Cory should be back soon with food and water for every one. Please, socialize and get to know one another until they arrive. I don't want to force y'all to sit and listen to me until you have eaten, so I won't start the sermon until after everyone has had a chance to get food."

The disciples guard was socializing with potential partners, as were some of the disciples. Azril was standing with Omegra observing the disciples converse, just as Cory's vehicle pulled up. Azril took a deep breath, embraced his connected partner, then led the disciples out to where Cory and Debora were unloading the vehicle.

"Please clean yourselves up and make sure you are wearing your uniform for dinner. Omegra and I are going to have everything set up for you when you are done," Azril told the disciples.

The disciples gathered around the watering troughs that had also been delivered with the shipping containers in order to wash up before heading to their housing assignments to change into their uniforms, as Azril walked over to help Cory. He was standing at the back of his SUV, unloading the pull trailer and retrieving things from behind the rear hatch.

Since they had moved onto the property that

morning and it was quickly approaching dinner time, Azril was feeling a little panicked. "Were you able to get everything we need for the first night and tomorrow morning?"

Cory reassured the leader. "Don't worry, Leader. We bought tables for everyone to sit at, we purchased disposable plates and cutlery, we even purchased everything we would need to take care of the disciples for the next few days. I promise, I will do everything I can to help you keep the City of Disciples operating, while you only think about the sermons and worship services."

Azril took a relaxing deep breath, as Omegra gently kissed his cheek, then proceeded to assist Cory with unloading the supplies from the back of his vehicle. After a few moments, a large box truck pulled onto the property.

"That's our dining tables," Cory informed.

Before the driver had exited the truck, a police car occupied by two officers pulled up onto the property. Azril and Cory approached the officers as the disciples stood by awaiting further instruction.

"Gentleman, I'm Officer Juarez and this is Officer Romero. We have a few questions to ask," the driver of the police car introduced, as they shook hands with the leader and Cory after exiting the vehicle.

"Absolutely officers. What can we do for you?" Azril asked.

"Early this morning, someone brought in some trash bags they said they got from this property," Officer Juarez informed.

"Trash bags? On this property? Well, good thing they took the garbage out before we purchased it," Cory said.

"When did you purchase this property? We just signed the papers at ten this morning," Azril told them.

"Are you able to prove that?" Officer Romero asked.

"Absolutely. Omegra, darling. Could you please retrieve the ownership papers for these nice officers?" Azril stated, turning his head to address his connected partner.

Omegra nodded and headed off to the leader's housing tent. It was only a minute later that she came jogging up with the packet of paper in her hand. She handed it directly to Officer Juarez, then kissed Azril on the cheek and backed away to join the other disciples.

Both officers flipped through the pages, nodding in agreement. Officer Juarez handed the packet to Azril. "Thank you, sir. I appreciate your cooperation. Sorry for bothering you fine folks."

"Can I ask what was in those trash bags? It

just seems a little strange that the police would have questions about plain old garbage," the leader inquired.

"Someone cut up a couple of bodies and placed the pieces in several trash bags," Officer Romero revealed.

"That is absolutely abhorrent. Why would someone do that?" Cory said, creating a disgusted look on his face.

Azril copied his disciples guard's facial expression. "And why would they just dump it here?"

"It was most likely dumped here because up until today, this has been an abandoned property. They most likely didn't think it would ever be found," Officer Juarez told them.

"Have you questioned the person who brought it to you?" Azril inquired.

"We have and we don't believe he has anything to do with the crime," Officer Romero informed him.

"If people are dumping dead bodies out here, we are going to need to put up a large gate along with a privacy fence all the way around this property," Azril told Cory, before turning to the officers. "Thank you for letting us know, officers. If we see any suspicious activity out here before we are able to protect the property, we will definitely give you a call."

The officers shook hands with Azril and Cory, before they returned to their police cruiser. As they drove off the property, the leader and his disciples guard returned to what they were doing before the interruption.

"Are we okay?" Omegra asked.

"We're fine. Just pretend it never happened and let's get the disciples fed," Azril told her.

The disciples began emerging from the housing circle, just as the driver of the box truck had exited the truck and stepped around to open the roll up door. Once contents of the vehicle were exposed, the disciples chipped in to assist the driver with unloading the tables.

Cory, Debora and Omegra had unloaded one hundred cases of water, one hundred fifty large pizzas and several boxes of canned goods in order to start the supply hoard. Azril stood off to the side with the dogs, as the disciples guard began setting up the tables and the disciples prepared the pizza and set up the plates, buffet style.

Twenty Four

Azril was so glad that Cory and Debora even thought to bring in tables for the disciples. The fact that they were assisting him in taking care of the disciples, had him realizing he had chosen the right tier one head disciples guard.

Omegra approached Azril, as the disciples cleaned up after eating. "I have something I need to discuss with you."

Azril was attempting to focus on the message for the worship service. "Can it wait until after the sermon?"

"Oh, absolutely," Omegra said, rubbing his shoulders.

The leader glanced over his notes, took a few deep breaths, then placed his hands on top of his connected partner's hands on his shoulders. Omegra stepped back, as he stood from the table where he had sat to eat.

Omegra followed him over to the tented sunroom. He sat down in the center of the tapestry that had been placed on the ground inside the sunroom. He bowed his head and recited the guidance prayer in a way for God to guide him in leading the disciples, as the disciples began gathering inside the worship area. Omegra pulled back the opening to the tent, so the disciples could see him clearly.

"Welcome to the City of Disciples," Azril began, after he prepared his position with his back straight and his hands placed on his knees. "Each and every one of you has contributed to the success of the City of Disciples. As long as you follow the Disciples Doctrine, you will always have a place here in the City of Disciples.

"I do see a few new faces here. Thank you to the outsiders who delivered the shipping containers, then chose to stay in order to hear the message of God as stated in the Disciples Doctrine. All of the work each of you do for the Disciples of God, will be compensated. Each week you will receive an envelope with a set amount of money, specific to you. Initially, everyone will make the same amount of money. As you recruit new disciples to live in the City of Disciples and they contribute to the finances, you will receive a bonus for each outsider as a thank you for your dedication to God.

"If the recruited disciple is shunned, the disciple who recruited them, will then be responsible to pay back the bonus received for that outsider. Please note, the highest level you are able to attain is level four. At that point, your pay will be capped off. You will still be able to recruit the outsiders, but you will be spending more time in the City of Disciples assisting the new disciples on how to recruit new disciples on their own. That is also the chain of command here in the City of Disciples.

"The chain of command would be the recruited disciple is to voice their concerns with the disciple who recruited them. Their concerns would move through the ranks up to the head disciples guard, depending upon which tier they are assigned. The head disciples guard will then bring those concerns to me, as the leader. I will then either address those concerns with the disciple personally, or give the solution to the disciples guard to relay to the disciple.

"Each of you will be assigned to the disciples guard tiers. There are three tiers with four disciples guards in each tier. Cory is the head of tier one, Danny is head of tier two and Martin is the head of tier three. Level four disciples can find any disciple in a grey uniform to take their concerns to.

"You are to have weekly meetings with your recruits to be sure that they understand what is expected of them. I am willing to initially meet the new disciples, due to the fact that in order for them to become a permanent disciple, they must participate in God's cleanse.

"Disciples are only issued a light blue uniform after they relinquish their funds from their previous life to the leader of the City of Disciples." Azril continued to explain the levels of pay and the purpose of the pay to the disciples, before he ended the worship service.

"I appreciate you taking the time to listen to this very important message that God has spoken through me. I am a Disciple of God and I will appease Him in worship."

"I am a Disciple of God and I will appease Him

in worship," all of the disciples mimicked, simultaneously.

Azril lowered his head and said a prayer to God, thanking Him for speaking through him, as the disciples retreated into their home tents and the outsiders purchased their copies of the Disciples Doctrine before leaving the city. Omegra, Cory, Danny and Martin were all waiting patiently for the leader to complete his prayer and raise his head.

"Okay, so what can I do for all of you?" Azril asked, as he stood up.

"I have something to discuss with you that I think might be helpful with the disciples," Omegra told him.

"I wanted to talk to you about some things that I feel might be helpful here in the City of Disciples," Cory let him know.

"I just wanted to know if there was anything else I could do for you, before I go to bed?" Danny asked.

"No Danny, thank you. You are dismissed," the leader told him, as he knelt down in front of Azril.

"I will be sure to have the tier two disciples guard up and ready to go at six in the morning," Danny said, as he stood and headed to his home tent.

"Okay Martin, what can I do for you?" Azril

asked.

"I would like to discuss the temporary isolation with Beatrice," Martin told Azril, looking down at his feet.

"I can understand, Martin. Don't be nervous to express your concerns. Please, join me inside," the leader told them.

The four of them walked back to the office area of the leader tent. Azril sat down on the floor and encouraged them to join him.

"Okay Omegra, you're up first," Azril said.

Omegra scooted closer to her connected partner and placed her hand on his knee. "I had an idea that we should set up some type of lake in order to proceed with God's cleanse, seeing as several of the disciples can already move up to level one and they haven't been changed out of the light blue uniform into the dark blue uniform."

"I'm intrigued. Tell me more," Azril wanted to know, as he tapped the tip of his finger to his chin.

Omegra continued excitedly. "Tonight, you spoke about the disciples recruiting new members. You mentioned that the outsiders who have relinquished their funds to the City of Disciples are the ones in the light blue uniforms. They aren't allowed to leave the City of Disciples to recruit outsiders until after God's cleanse and they receive their dark blue uniforms. What if we create a lake here in the City of Disciples? Sara, Debora and Emma have already brought in several outsiders who have also relinquished their funds, for the three of them to go straight into the green uniform."

"That's a great idea. I know Emma has been making the dark blue uniforms for that purpose, but do you know if she has been making any of the others?" Azril asked her.

"She has been able to make one thousand of each color, except the black and grey. She made twenty of the black, so we have ten each. As for the grey, she made a hundred and twenty for each of the disciples guard to also have ten each," she told him.

"That's amazing! How has she been able to make so many in such a short period of time?" Azril wondered.

"She said that she told her fashion design professor that she was starting a business and had her first client, but she needed help producing the order. The professor gave the pattern to the rest of the class and that is all they did for two days," Omegra said.

"She is very resourceful and I'm glad she is part of the disciples. As for the lake, find out if any of the disciples guard, as well as the disciples, have any experience in that specific field in order to make sure that it's not just a mud hole," Azril told Omegra, before she stepped out of the tent and he turned toward Cory. "Okay Cory, you're up. What can I do for you?"

"I think we need to get canopies or something to cover over the open areas where the disciples gather, just incase it rains," Cory mentioned.

"I'm okay with getting some type of covering for the eating and worship areas, but other than that, they can just hunker down inside their housing tents," the leader told Cory, then turned toward Martin, as Cory stepped out of the tent. "Okay Martin, what do you have for me?"

"I understand that Beatrice is in isolation for committing several evil acts within the City of Disciples, but are we able to place a covering over the temporary isolation area?" Martin asked.

"Is there a problem with her being exposed? Is it specifically for weather related protection?" Azril wondered.

Martin took a deep breath and tried to explain his concerns carefully. "Well no. The problem is her disruptions. She yells out to any of the disciples that are close enough to hear her and she is trying to convince everyone that she was initially chosen as your connected partner, but Omegra swept in and stole you from her. I feel like the covering will keep her from trying to get the attention of others if she can't see them."

Azril nodded in agreement. "Martin, you absolutely have my permission to place the tarp from my original shelter over the isolation chamber. Also, could you please let Tom and Walter know that I would like to see them."

"Thank you, Leader. I will get them now," Martin said, before bowing in front of the leader for blessing, then exiting the tent.

As soon as Azril was left alone, he took a deep, cleansing breath and waited for Tom and Walter. It wasn't long before they arrived.

"Leader, Martin said you wanted to see us," Tom said, as they stepped into the leader tent.

The two of them were suppose to be keeping an eye on the isolated disciple, but Azril was a little frustrated that they were unable to keep her from disrupting the City of Disciples. "Yes. Martin will be placing a covering over the isolation cage that Beatrice is being held in, because he has informed me that she is yelling out to the other disciples. As well as disrupting the peaceful nature of the City of Disciples. Haven't y'all been keeping an eye on her?"

"We have been taking turns going over there. Yes, she is yelling out inappropriate things and incorrect statements, but we didn't see anything wrong with it," Walter said, shrugging it off.

Azril was disappointed with their nonchalant response to the situation. "At least Martin came up with a solution. The two of you are now assigned to six hour shifts each. Tom, you will be taking the first shift. Grab a chair and head over to the isolation area. All you are going to do for the first three hours is sit next to the isolation cage and keep an eye on her. I will send another disciples guard over there to relieve you for half an hour to take a break. After that thirty minutes, you are to go back over and sit for another three hours. After that, Walter will come over to relieve you. Walter, you will do the same thing. She is only to be in isolation for seven days, but after her disruptive behavior, she is now getting another three days placed on her isolation."

"This is our job assignment for the next ten days?" Tom asked.

"Yes. That means that when you are not on your six hour shift, you are eating, bathing and sleeping. I know the two of you have been conversing with a couple of disciples as potential connected partners, but for the next ten days your only focus needs to be on your job assignment," the leader said.

"Is there going to be job assignments to the isolation chambers when the permanent isolation and housing is built?" Walter wanted to know.

Azril felt like the two of them were being petulant. "No. The permanent isolation will be locked down like solitary in a prison, so we won't need any disciples guards assigned to watch them. I will also have cameras in the area that I can watch from not only my office, but also from my housing unit. Now, go take your post and I will speak with the other disciples guard."

Tom headed over to the isolation where Martin was draping the tarp over the cage, as Beatrice screamed at him. Walter entered his housing tent and waited for his shift.

Azril exited his housing tent and located David and Stephen. "I have assigned Tom and Walter to six hour shifts at the isolation area. They are to receive a thirty minute lunch break. Would the two of you be willing to cover the isolation post during Tom and Walter's breaks?"

They both agreed, then the leader found his connected partner, so he could retire for the night. They went into their tent room and knelt down on the floor next to their bed to pray just before they went to sleep.

"At the end of this day, I thank you for all the guidance I have received from you. I hope I have made choices pleasing to you. I have done what I could to be the leader you have chosen for me to be and can only do what is best for me. Please protect me through this night as I dream of your Promised Land. I am a Disciple of God and I will appease You in worship," Azril and Omegra recited the evening prayer together.

Twenty Five

The next morning, when Azril and Omegra woke up in the City of Disciples, the leader decided to hold his connected partner for a few moments, before they rolled out of the bed and sat down on the floor to pray, in order to start their day.

Azril and Omegra knelt down next to their bed and recited the morning prayer. "Because you have given it to me, God, I will begin this day. I thank you for watching over me during the night. I will do my best to lead the disciples with your teachings today in order to please You and in accordance with Your guidance. Please dear God, watch over me as I go through this day and take care of me. I am a Disciple of God and I will appease You in worship."

As the leader and his connected partner stepped out of their housing tent, Azril took a deep breath and could smell eggs and bacon cooking, along with a sweet scent he thought could be either pancakes or waffles. They stepped between their tent and the tent next to it, out of the worship circle and emerged next to the area where the tables were set up. Several disciples, along with Martin, were cooking breakfast for the entire City of Disciples with a very extravagant outdoor kitchen grill.

Azril yawned and approached Martin. "Where did this come from?"

"One of the new disciples brought it with them and felt as though we could use something to cook on," Martin informed.

"New disciples? Did we get more since last night?" Azril wondered.

"We sure did. Bright and early this morning, just before the sun came up, Cory and Danny were preparing the disciples guard to start the day and five vehicles pulled up. They relinquished their funds to Cory and had this entire outdoor kitchen cooking grill on the back of one of the trucks," Martin told him.

"I don't understand how they got here," Azril inquired.

Martin flipped the pancakes on the griddle. "Sharon got up with the disciples guard and decided to go over to the college campus to grab Beatrice's laptop in order to bring it back here for you. In that process, she also decided to grab anything else that could be sold in order to contribute to the funds of the City of Disciples. There were several students wandering around the campus and she decided to ask if they wanted to purchase anything. When they asked her why she was selling all of the stuff she had, she told them about the disciples. She said that she had read the Converting Outsiders chapter from the Disciples Doctrine to them and immediately they wanted to join her."

"Where is Sharon?" Azril asked.

"She is in her housing tent logging the funds into something she called a spreadsheet," Martin told him.

"What is a spreadsheet and how does it log the funds?" Azril asked him.

"It's some type of computer program. I'm not sure how it works, but she said to let you know, so you could go in and collect the funds that were relinquished this morning," Martin said.

"Thank you, Martin," Azril said, patting him on the shoulder before walking back to the housing tents to meet with Sharon.

Sharon looked up at Azril, as he entered her tent. "Leader, I created a worksheet for the disciples guard. I figured that they needed a way to log funds when random disciples show up in the City of Disciples. The disciple starts the worksheet, by writing down their name and the amount they brought in with them. That way when the disciples guard confirms the amount, it should basically match."

Azril was amazed at how much she had accomplished. "Wow, okay. I really appreciate that. Martin said you were creating a spreadsheet to log the funds."

Sharon turned the laptop, so the leader could see the screen. "I did. I thought it would be easier for you to keep track of funds coming in and expenses going out on a spreadsheet."

"I'm not sure what a spreadsheet is, or what it does, so I'm going to need you to go over it with Omegra and see what she says about it," Azril told her. "I'll go get her and send her over."

Azril felt overwhelmed by the thought of anything related to computers, so he wanted to pass it off to his connected partner. He approached Omegra, as she sat enjoying a plate of pancakes and eggs and told her about Sharon's spreadsheet.

Omegra swallowed the food in her mouth. "Oh, okay. I'll be right back. I'm going to see if she wants to go over it with me while we eat."

"You stay here. I'll get her and have her come out here to you," Azril told her, heading back to the housing tents. "Sharon, have you had any breakfast yet?"

Sharon placed her hand on her stomach as it grumbled. "Actually, I haven't. I have been working on this all morning and I haven't even thought about it."

"Omegra is having breakfast right now. She wanted to know if you would like to join her and discuss the finances with her over breakfast," Azril told her.

Sharon closed the laptop and stood. "That sounds perfect. By the way, do you know when we will be getting electricity out here?"

"I'm going to have Cory call the electric company to come out here and install power as soon as they are able to. Why do you ask?" Azril wondered.

"Debora says the walkie talkies they got have to be charged and I don't know how much longer the battery is going to last on the laptop," Sharon informed.

Azril accompanied Sharon over to the eating area. "As soon as I know, I will let you know."

Martin approached the leader with a paper plate full of food. "Leader, I made you a plate with five pancakes, two eggs and three pieces of bacon."

"Thank you Martin. You are an asset to the disciples guard and the City of Disciples," the leader told him, taking the plate. "Where is Cory and Danny?"

"They are standing outside your housing tent with the new disciples. Cory placed the funds inside your tent and decided to stand guard, then Danny showed the new disciples who showed up this morning around the property before he took them over there to wait for their housing and job assignments along with receiving a uniform," Martin told him.

"I will need to get with Emma for them to get a uniform. She is holding them in her housing tent as her job assignment when we get the permanent housing building. Also, do you happen to know if the professionally printed and bound copies of the Disciples Doctrine have arrived?"

Azril asked.

"Yes, Sharon brought them back with her from the dorms. She has them in her housing tent and passed out the official copies to all of the disciples who have the temporary copies. She also made a plan to keep an inventory count of the Disciples Doctrine each week so she could order more before we run out," Martin told him.

Azril placed his hand on Martin's head for blessing. "All of you disciples have been so helpful and shown loyalty to the City of Disciples, I might need to issue bonuses to those of you who have gone above and beyond to get us up and running. Thank you, Martin."

Azril took his breakfast and headed over toward his housing tent. Cory and Danny were standing guard out front with the new disciples sitting in the worship area asking questions about the disciples.

"Cory, thank you so much. Danny, I appreciate your initiative. Welcome new disciples," Azril said, as he approached them.

Azril blessed each new disciple as he walked past them, then turned to enter the sunroom area of his housing tent. Azril sat down next to six bags that had been placed off to the side, just inside of the opening. As he got comfortable, the leader picked up a piece of bacon from his plate and began eating.

Cory crouched in front of the leader and whispered. "We netted over four million with these new disciples."

"That's amazing. Would that put us up to almost half a billion?" Azril whispered to Cory.

"Not with what we have spent already on the City of Disciples, but Sharon has the exact amount on the computer thingy she made," Cory told him.

Azril raised his voice, just enough, for the new disciples to hear him. "Once we get the shipping containers buried, with at least two hatch doors in two separate containers, I will need you to put together a group of disciples who have the skills to build. Those will be the disciples who will assist in building the permanent housing unit. I have an idea of how I want it, but I will need someone who can create a blue print and direct the disciples to build it to my specs."

One of the new disciples stood up. "I'm actually an architect major and can assist you with that."

"Why don't we start with getting to know each other first," Azril said. "Some of my story is actually in the Disciples Doctrine, so you can find out about me there. So tell me your name and a little bit about yourself and what brought you here."

"I'm Mitchell," the architect major began. "I have three months before graduation and I will receive my degree. I have applied to over a hundred architect firms and they only want experienced architects. I can't gain experience without being hired and my professor basically told me I could either go on to start my own architectural firm, or become an architect professor. I feel like I just spent the last four years of my life wasting time before I go flip burgers at a fast food joint.

"I saw Sharon on the front lawn of the dorms at the butt crack of dawn and started talking to her. She told me she was selling a bunch of shit for the City of Disciples and I was intrigued. She read some stuff from the Disciples Doctrine and I decided to leave the struggle of trying to find a job behind. She told me that you might need help with designing a few buildings, so I took all my shit over to a pawn shop and sold everything I owned, except my truck. Now I'm here and I can't wait to help you design the buildings you require to make the City of Disciples functional."

Mitchell was going prematurely grey. Parts of the original black color of his hair showed through the silver streaks that were beginning to take over.

"Thank you, Mitchell. I'm looking forward to working with you. Also, please watch the profanity in your speech," Azril told him.

"I'm Mark. I was with Mitchell when we met Sharon this morning. I'm actually a licensed electrician, but I'm having the same problem as Mitchell with finding a job."

Mark had dark brown hair that was feathered just below his ears. He was dressed in a way that suggested he wasn't opposed to getting dirty while working hard.

"We could use you as well with setting up some of the buildings. I'm glad you're here," Azril told him.

"I'm Jordan. The five of us have known each other since high school. We basically do everything together and that's really the only reason why I'm here. Although, while we were sitting here asking Cory and Danny a few questions about the disciples, I'm actually excited to be here."

Jordan was well groomed and seemed to be focused on his appearance. When he spoke, he looked around the area and never once looked in the direction of the leader.

Azril felt there was something off about Jordan, but he would give him the benefit of the doubt. "Well, I hope you will be happy here."

"I'm Kyle. I'm the oldest of the five of us. I was a senior in high school when they were freshman. I watched out for them because they were bullied by the other seniors. I went off to medical school, but stayed in touch with these guys. I had just finished my residency and was thinking about opening my own medical practice in a small town. I was visiting the guys at the college when we met Sharon. I figured you could need a doctor here in the City of Disciples."

Kyle held himself in a professional manner. Azril felt that he could be caring and that he was willing to help the disciples.

"We are actually planning on putting the medical building in the center of the property. I think you would be a perfect fit. Thank you, Kyle," Azril said.

"I'm Justin. I went to the same specialty college as Mark, except I'm a licensed plumber. I can't get work and at least twice a week, these guys are having to drag my drunk ass off a random park bench that I passed out on."

Justin was disheveled, from his hair to his clothing. He gave off the appearance that he was giving up on life and the City of Disciples was his last chance.

"You could be useful in the construction of the buildings as well. Welcome Justin," Azril said.

"Are we going to get temporary bathroom facilities?" Danny asked, as Azril finished the breakfast he had eaten while the new disciples introduced themselves.

"Yes, let me get you some money and you can go purchase camping supplies. Cory, have you had the chance to contact the utility companies, so we can get water, septic and electric service out here?" Azril asked.

"I was actually able to do that yesterday. We are scheduled for the end of the week to get electricity set up. The beginning of next week, we will have the water well dug and the end of next week, we will have the septic system installed," Cory told him.

"Ya'll are amazing," Azril said, as he stood up and acknowledged his head disciples guard. "I'm so glad the five of you have decided to join us here in the City of Disciples. I will have Disciple Emma come over to get y'all set up with the beginner uniforms."

Twenty Six

After the disciples had been on the property for a couple of months, Cory was able to get a crane to come into the City of Disciples and place the shipping containers down into the holes that had been dug. The disciples had acquired lawn maintenance equipment and cleared out the part of the property where Azril wanted to place the housing unit building. Jerry and Lawerence had welding experience, so they were creating the hatch doors in the top of the containers after they were placed into the ground.

Cory and Mitchell were brainstorming and making rough drawings of the housing and worship building from the ideas that Azril had verbalized. Mitchell was able to come up with seven different drawings of what the building would look like from the outside.

Azril wanted to see his vision for the inside of the building, so he sat down with Mitchell and gave him several notes of what he wanted each housing unit to look like. The leader had chosen the drawing of the outside of the building that he felt was the closest to his vision.

Mitchell took the notes from Azril and created a three dimensional model of what the inside of the building would look like. As well, he had created a blueprint of what the leader wanted. Azril approved it and Mitchell made a list of materials he would need, which was passed to Cory who would price it out for funds.

Omegra, Cory, Danny and Azril were all inspecting the hatches, as Jerry and Lawerence installed the steps in order to get down into the containers. The leader jumped down on top of the containers and walked around, trying to figure out the size and layout.

"Danny, you had a great idea. I'm glad that you suggested putting the hatches on two different ends, so the far end will only be accessible from my office, directly under my living quarters and the other end will only be accessible from the worship area for the disciples," Azril mentioned.

Cory crouched down to get closer to the leader. "Jerry and Lawrence said they would only remove the walls in order to connect these two shipping containers and those three. That way, the two that are for the isolation chambers will be one large area and the other three that are for the supply hoard will be one large area."

Azril nodded with affirmation. "Perfect, this is coming together nicely."

"What the fuck, bitch! Get in the fucking car. I have been looking for you for over a month," a deep voice boomed across the property.

Azril stepped over to the edge and reached out for Danny and Cory to assist him off the containers. The four of them ran across the property to quickly arrive to where the yelling was coming from. Omegra approached Martin for safety, as the leader stepped up in front of the outsider who was yelling. He put his hand in front of the outsider's face, in order to get him to stop screaming.

"What the fuck, man," the outsider said.

"Excuse me, I'm going to need you to stop

yelling and stop using profanity within the City of Disciples," Azril told the outsider.

The outsider stepped up to the leader's face and yelled. "Fuck you, dip shit! I want Samantha! She just disappeared over a month ago without telling anyone!"

"Lonny, please stop yelling. I came here to escape. I like it here and you need to leave," Samantha calmly told the outsider.

"Naw, bitch!" Lonny told Samantha, then slapped her across the face. "Get in the car! You're coming back with me! You're pregnant with my baby and your family has already agreed that we are going to get married!"

"Cory, Danny, get him," Azril said, as Sharon stepped up behind Samantha.

Lonny held up his fists in a fight stance. "The fuck you are! Get the fuck away from me!"

Cory and Danny tried grabbing Lonny's arms. The outsider shoved Danny and gave Cory time to step up behind him. The tier one disciples guard hooked his arms under Lonny's arm pits and interlocked his fingers behind the outsider's neck, incapacitating him.

Azril stepped up next to his disciple and wrapped his right arm over her shoulders. "Samantha, would you like this outsider shunned from the physical land just as God will shun him

261

from the promised land?"

"Yes please." Tears were streaming down her face, as she placed her hand to her cheek where Lonny had slapped her. "I would also appreciate a personal prayer session with you."

"Thank you," Azril told her, placing his hand on her forehead for a blessing.

The leader lowered his arm. He also gave Sharon a blessing as she comforted Samantha.

Azril directed the head disciples guard to follow behind him. "Bring him this way."

The outsider argued, as Cory forced him to follow Azril. "This is bull shit! You can't do shit to me!"

Azril was glad that Beatrice managed to behave herself after spending ten days in isolation. The cage had been empty for about six weeks. The leader stepped toward the back of the property where the temporary isolation cage had been placed. As Cory and Danny tried stuffing Lonny into the isolation cage, the outsider fought.

"I'm not going in that fucking cage!" Lonny stiffened his legs and made it difficult to stuff his six foot three inch height into the three foot tall isolation chamber.

Azril shrugged. "If he is refusing to be put in the cage, we will just shun him now. That just means he doesn't get the opportunity to reflect on his actions and change his mind."

Beatrice ran up behind them and she was livid by Azril's response. "Leader, I find it unfair that you are willing to give the outsider more respect than you would a disciple."

"Beatrice, don't you have a job assignment that you are suppose to be doing?" Azril asked her.

The disciple decided to argue with him. "This is the first person that you have placed in the isolation chamber since I was caged and I wanted to make sure it was actually going to happen."

"This has nothing to do with you, bitch!" Lonny told her.

The outsider lunged toward her. Luckily, Cory and Danny had a firm grip on him. They slammed him on the ground, face first. Cory placed his knee on Lonny's back and wrenched his left arm straight back.

Beatrice placed her hands on her hips. "I can be wherever I want to be. I am a Disciple of God and I have free rein of this property."

"Beatrice, you need to go back to your job assignment," Azril instructed.

"No, I want to watch you stuff him into that cage," Beatrice ordered.

"If you don't go back with the other disciples now, you will be placed back into the isolation chamber," Azril warned her.

"You're going to lose the respect of your disciples if you don't place that outsider in isolation," Beatrice said, as she turned and walked back through the property.

"They are the Disciples of God, not my disciples," the leader told her.

Beatrice waved her hand over her shoulder, as if she was done responding to the leader. Cory and Danny lifted the outsider up onto his feet. They dragged him back through the property, following behind Azril.

The leader tried to stay close to Beatrice to ensure she went back to her job assignment. As they arrived back to where all the disciples were gathered, Azril guided Cory and Danny to take Lonny over to an open area where they could perform the shunning.

"Disciples, due to the resistance of the outsider, we are going to move the shunning ceremony to now," Azril said, addressing the entire City of Disciples.

Omegra and Martin went around and collected all of the tools that the disciples were working with, so they could head over to the first shunning on the new property. Cory and Danny forced Lonny onto his knees as the rest of the disciples guard lined up next to them - five next to Cory and Five next to Danny.

The disciples gathered around to witness the shunning. Omegra stood next to Azril with Sharon and Samantha next to her. The leader pulled out his butterfly knife. He flipped the knife open and stepped up into the outsider's face.

Azril began the shunning ceremony. "We are gathered here to witness the shunning of this outsider from the physical land, just as God will shun him from the promised land. He is guilty of disrespect of God and the leader of the City of Disciples, as well as placing his hands on a disciple with the intent to inflict harm. For each offense he has committed against the disciples, he will be bled of his wrong doings before being released from the physical land. Samantha, please step forward. If you wish, you may assist in the shunning."

Samantha took the knife and slowly ran the blade along each side of Lonny's face, gashing each on of his cheeks. "You violated me and that is how I became pregnant. We were never together. It is your fault I left home. You convinced my parents that we were in a loving relationship and this baby was conceived in love. This baby was conceived without consent. I took the baby to get away from you."

Lonny spit at Samantha. "Fuck you! You don't

even know the whole story!"

"So tell me the story," Samantha requested, placing the blade of the knife under his chin.

"Technically, your parents put us together before you were born. When your mother was pregnant with you, I was three and my parents were friends with your parents. They had promised that when you turned fifteen, we were suppose to start dating. Unfortunately, when I was ten and you were seven, my dad was relocated with his job and we moved away. I knew that when I turned eighteen, I was suppose to move back closer to you in order to claim what was mine," Lonny admitted.

"That's why you have been around for the past couple of years?" Samantha asked.

"Yes. I was told that you knew. Your parents encouraged me to claim you and force you to be connected to me forever. When they found out you were pregnant, they felt as though they had finally fulfilled your prophesy," Lonny told her.

"You're lying," Samantha said, as she ran the knife across his chest, through his shirt. "First, you have never spoken to me with the sweet tone you have now and second, my parents told that story differently," Samantha told him.

"You're a dumb bitch. The fact that you would believe the two people who sold you when you were only a fetus and not me. I have spent my entire life waiting for the time that we could be together," the outsider responded.

"Finish it," Samantha told the leader, as she turned her back to Lonny and passed the knife back to Azril.

"This outsider is now to be shunned," Azril told the disciples.

The leader turned toward the outsider and nodded his head. Cory and Danny lifted Lonny to his feet. The outsider used the head disciples guard as leverage, kicking his legs at the leader. Azril was quick enough to get out of the way from being struck by Lonny's feet.

Cory and Danny slammed him on the ground, face down, just as they had before. Cory decided to zip tie each one of Lonny's legs to the head disciples guard. Lonny's right leg to Cory's left leg and Lonny's left leg to Danny's right leg.

Once he was subdued, Cory and Danny lifted him back up onto his feet. As soon as they had the outsider settled, Azril didn't hesitate as he plunged the knife into the outsider's abdomen.

With Lonny, the leader started just above his shaft and pulled the knife up his body until it stopped at his ribcage. The outsider collapsed onto the ground after Azril pulled the knife out of his body. Azril stood over Lonny and watched him gasp for air and bleed out, while Cory and Danny cut off the zip ties around their ankles.

After a few moments, Azril turned to face the disciples and finish off the shunning ceremony. "God of wisdom and leader of the promised land, we bring before you the shunning of an outsider who has gone against the City of Disciples and against You. Just as we have shunned him from the physical land, You will shun him from the promised land. Be with all disciples as we forget about the shunned outsider and continue to look toward You. We are Disciples of God and we will appease You in worship."

"We are Disciples of God and we will appease You in worship," the disciples mimicked, simultaneously.

The disciples turned and headed back to their work assignments, as the disciples guard - minus Martin - began digging the shunning pit. Azril, Omegra, Martin Sharon and Samantha headed back to the leader tent. As they entered the sunroom area, Samantha and Sharon knelt in front of the leader for blessing.

Azril blessed both disciples. "Sharon, could you please go with Omegra and Martin. I think Samantha might benefit from some one on one time."

The disciple nodded and stepped out of the

sunroom area of the leader's tent with the leader's connected partner. Azril and Samantha moved into the center of the tent and sat down on the meditation rug. Azril held Samantha's hands and bowed his head, reciting a prayer for her.

"God, we have problems and pressures that are overwhelming. I am teaching the disciples to seek You in troubling times. The outsiders are mocking your teachings and we are having trouble keeping the evil outsiders from coming into the City of Disciples. Take away our guilt and failure and reassure us that this trouble is only temporary. Give us the joy that comes from learning about the promised land and know that our time in the physical land is limited. Renew our devotion for You and the knowledge that without You we would be lost. I am a Disciple of God and I will appease You in worship."

"I am a Disciple of God and I will appease You in worship," Samantha repeated.

Twenty Seven

Azril looked up, made direct eye contact with Samantha and quietly stared at her for a few moments before speaking. She had tears streaming down her face.

"You don't have to worry about Lonny anymore. He has been shunned from the physical land," the leader told her.

"What about my baby?" she asked.

Azril rubbed Samantha's knuckles with his thumbs. "We are all here for anything you need. The storage containers will be stocked with the necessary items needed for everyone here in the City of Disciples; that includes your baby."

Samantha squeezed his hands. "Am I still going to get medical care for me and my baby here within the City of Disciples, or do I need to go out and find an outsider doctor?"

"We will have a medical facility, here in the City of Disciples and we are in the process of recruiting medical staff. We do have one disciple that is a doctor who is wanting to open a small, personal practice and he is looking forward to working with the disciples. You won't need to leave for any reason, unless it's needed," the leader told her.

Samantha kissed the back of his hands, one at a time. "Thank you, Leader. I appreciate you and the City of Disciples. I pray that I am worthy to stay here in the physical land, so that God may receive me into the promised land."

"You are valuable to the physical land, as well as the City of Disciples. God will find favor with you in the promised land. You shall find a connected partner within the disciples in order to help expand your family. Did you want to tell me anything? You said he lied about the story as to how the two of you were connected. Would you like to tell me about that?" Azril asked.

Samantha took a deep breath and prepared to tell her story. "My parents told me that they were friends with his parents. Immediately, when my mother became pregnant, his mother said that I was to belong to her son. My parents didn't even know if I was a boy or a girl at the time and it made them uneasy that his mother used the words that I was to BELONG to him. It was as if I was property and not a person.

"Lonny is three and a half years older than I am. When I was two and he was five, my mother told me that he forced me to lay down and he was touching me inappropriately. That's when my parents decided to move away from them to keep me safe.

"One day when I was fifteen, he was eighteen, Lonny showed up at my parent's house. He told my parents that he was going to college close by and he found out that we were around and wanted to know if he could stay with us. He was so nice and respectful, they figured that he had changed as he got older. We had moved away from him when he was five and they assumed he had moved on, so they let him stay with us.

"Apparently, he was in constant communication with his parents the entire time. They were talking him through how to gain the trust of my parents in order to take advantage of me. He waited until my seventeenth birthday, then he snuck into my room every day for a week and told me that we were destined to be connected forever because I belonged to him.

"When I finally told my mother what he had done, I was pregnant. Lonny told my parents we would get married and be a happy family. They didn't know what to do, so they agreed that once I graduated from high school, I was to marry Lonny. I protested the union, but my father told me that if I didn't marry him I would have to give up the baby.

"That's when I left home. I found Beth, who has been my best friend since I was thirteen. She is a year older than me and came to this college where she had met Sara and Debora. They told her about the disciples and she told me about the disciples. When I told her the problem I was having, she brought me here. Since I have been here, I have felt calm, loved and at peace. That was until Lonny showed up and kicked up my fear. It doesn't matter how my baby was conceived, I just want to protect her. I didn't ask to be violated, but she didn't ask to be forced to be here. She deserves a chance to live and only feel love." Samantha wiped the tears from her cheeks.

"So you know you're having a girl?" Azril

asked.

"No, but I just have that feeling," Samantha admitted, wrapping her arms around her stomach.

Azril placed his hand on her head for blessing. "Thank you, Samantha. I am so glad you are here."

Omegra entered the tent and assisted Samantha into a standing position. She escorted the disciple out of the tent, as Azril remained on the meditation rug, praying for Samantha to find a connected partner within favor of God. Omegra returned and waited for the leader to finish his prayer.

"God, as Samantha walks through this day that You have given us, but she is alone. We all trust in the love You have for us, but she needs help to find someone for her in the physical land to love as much. Show her the way to love others so they may love her back. She is patient and is willing to wait for You to bring them to her. She is ready to serve them with the gifts You have given her. We are Disciples of God and we will appease You in worship," Azril prayed.

Omegra knelt down next to him. "She is going to have to work hard to find favor with God due to becoming one flesh with someone before she was connected. Is she able to find a connected partner when she has a child from someone she wasn't connected to?"

Azril explained the situation to his connected partner. "Technically, she was taken advantage of. What happened to her is in the Disciples Doctrine in the connected partners chapter. Each disciple who is able to give birth to a child, must be willing to incubate that child and take care of that child for no less than twenty one years. If the disciple did not choose for the seed to take hold, nor are they ready to take the responsibility of the child, it is at the discretion of the disciple as to the decision of their own body.

"That means that she did not do anything wrong and she is able to make the choice to keep the baby and find a disciple for a connected partner. The one who violated her was shunned due to the evil acts he committed, so she is clear to find a connected partner here within the City of Disciples. I am going to try to connect her with one of my disciples guard. Cory and Danny have already found partners. I have also seen Martin talking to Farrah secretly, along with Tom and Walter have been talking to a couple of disciples."

Omegra nodded, as she understood. "I would love it if the disciples guard were to participate in a connection ceremony within the next two weeks. That would make it easier to assign housing units to connected partners rather than a bunch of single disciples when the housing and worship building is completed."

"It will probably be at least a year before the building will be completed. I will definitely approach Cory and Danny and find out if they believe Sara and Debora are ready to be connected partners," Azril said.

"Each disciple is in the light blue uniform right now except you and I are in black and the disciples guard in grey. In order for the disciples to become connected partners, don't they have to be on the same level?" Omegra inquired.

Azril nodded. "That is true. At this point, everyone who has contributed to the City of Disciples needs to participate in God's cleanse before we perform any connection ceremonies. Since the disciples, as of now, are on the same level as the disciples guard, they can be connected partners."

"Once we get the disciples through God's cleanse and they move into the dark blue uniforms, then we can get the disciples guard through God's cleanse," Omegra said.

"I would prefer it if the disciples guard went through God's cleanse first. It would help to know that they are loyal to the City of Disciples," Azril told her.

"That sounds like a perfect plan." Omegra

stood and continued. "On another note, I believe I have found a couple of disciples who are able to create a pond for God's cleanse. They just need your guidance as to where you want it on the property and how big you want it."

Azril stood up, so he look her in her eyes. "I can do that. I will have disciples guard tier one go get some lawn steaks and ribbon to mark off where the buildings are going to go, so we can find the right place for the cleansing pond."

"Azril, we need to talk," Beatrice said, barging into the leader tent.

Omegra stood between the disciple and her connected partner. "You are no longer in favor with God. As soon as the permanent isolation chambers are completed, your housing assignment will begin there. You are going to need to re-familiarize yourself with the Disciples Doctrine. Your offering has already been rejected and you are to only refer to him as leader. As well, due to your behavior, when the other disciples go through God's cleanse, you will not be allowed to participate."

Beatrice ignored Omegra and addressed Azril. "I knew I was being singled out. You have other disciples who are being disrespectful and yet, I'm the one who keeps getting placed in isolation."

"Get out!" Azril yelled, retrieving the walkie

talkie that had been left in his tent, in order to contact the disciples guard. He pressed the button and spoke into the speaker. "Tom, Walter, this is Azril. Come back."

"This is Tom. Walter is right here with me. Go ahead, Leader," a voice came through the radio.

"Could the two of you please meet me in my housing tent?" Azril told him.

"Yes sir. We will be right there," he responded.

As Azril waited for the two disciples guard to arrive, Omegra stood her ground between the leader and the disciple. She wanted to make sure that Beatrice didn't try putting her hands on him.

Twenty Eight

Tom and Walter arrived and entered the leader's housing tent. They immediately knew what he wanted. They grabbed Beatrice and pulled her out of the sunroom area, as she struggled under their grasp.

Beatrice kicked her legs and straightened her arms to get away. "I'm not going back in that cage. The leader and I are meant to be together.

God led me here to him."

Tom and Walter dropped Beatrice on the ground in the worship circle. Azril and Omegra followed the disciples guard out of the tent. The leader motioned for them to pick her up and follow him toward the isolation area.

Beatrice yelled, as she was dragged through the property. "I refuse to be caged again!"

"Don't worry, Beatrice. The new isolation chambers are ready," Tom said.

"Were they able to figure out the air circulation, as well as the central air situation down there?" Azril asked.

Walter had to shout over Beatrice's screaming. "Yes, as a matter of fact, they figured it out earlier this afternoon before the shunning."

Beatrice repeated the same thing over and over the entire way to isolation. "STOP! LET ME GO! I'M THE LEADER'S CONNECTED PARTNER!"

As they stepped up to the shipping container hatch that led down to the isolation chambers, Lawerence and Jerry were waiting at the top of the stairs. It would be the first time that Azril had been inside the isolation containers since they had been completed.

Jerry motioned for Azril to join Lawerence and him down inside the shipping containers. "Leader, we were able to fit ten isolation chambers down-stairs. Five in one container, five in the other and a hallway down the middle. We made sure to expedite the construction in order to contain the one disciple who can't seem to learn boundaries."

Lawerence disappeared down the stairs first, followed by Jerry, then Azril. Tom led Beatrice down with Walter behind her. Omegra decided to head back to join the other disciples.

At the bottom of the stairs, the entire isolation area was white, in order to give the illusion of more space than there actually was. There was a hook on the wall at the bottom of the staircase, where a master key for all of the isolation chambers hung. Each door had a small circular window at the perfect hight for Azril to be able to see in. At the bottom of each door was a hatch with a latched closure in order to slide in plates of food for the isolated disciples and outsiders.

On the wall, just before each door was a hook, with a clipboard hanging. There was a note sheet on the clipboard, just to keep track of which disciple or outsider was in each isolation chamber. Azril was amazed with the outside of the rooms. He used the key to open isolation chamber number one and just inside was a metal framed bed with a foam mattress, pillow and thin blanket. In one far corner there was a commode with a curtain that pulled around it for privacy; in the other far corner was a single stall shower with a rounded, frosted, sliding door.

"This is awesome. Now the isolated disciple, or outsider has their own facilities to use. Is there any water hooked up in here?" Azril asked, as Tom and Walter shoved Beatrice to the floor into room number one and the leader locked the door behind her.

"As a matter of fact, they were able to get that hooked up before the air conditioning was completed. They are set up with timed lights and in-door plumbing," Jerry admitted.

"What is the timer on the lights for?" Azril asked the disciples guard.

Lawerence showed Azril the timer box hanging on the wall near the stairs. "When the sun comes up, the lights turn on. When the sun goes down, the lights turn off. We even have them set up to dim on or off depending upon sunrise, or sunset. We thought that would give them more of a sense of how long they had been locked up."

"Since the building hasn't been erected yet, does anyone have to guard Beatrice while she is down here?" Tom asked.

Azril shook his head. "No. The locks on the doors, as well as the top hatch should be enough security to keep her down here. Plus, I'm thinking about having baby monitor cameras setup in here, so I can watch the isolated disciples or outsiders before the surveillance cameras are installed when the building is finished."

Walter sighed with relief. "Thank goodness. I don't know how much more of her whining I could take. All she did for most of the ten days we were having to watch her for was bitch and complain."

"Thank you Tom and Walter, for your dedicated service to the City of Disciples. You both are appreciated," Azril told them.

"I am a Disciple of God and I will appease Him in worship," Walter said, kneeling in front of Azril and bowing his head for blessing.

Tom and Walter headed up the stairs and out of the isolation area, leaving Azril with Jerry and Lawerence. The leader was thinking about what his connected partner had said about the disciples guard all having connected partners.

Azril wanted to find out if Jerry and Lawerence were thinking about any disciples for connection, without actually asking. "Samantha is pregnant and without a connected partner, or a partner of any kind. The way the outsider approached her about the baby, shows that her family may be a threat to the City of Disciples. Someone will need to keep an eye on her to ensure that she is safe and no outsider sneaks into the confines of the city for malicious intent."

"I'll do it," Lawerence spoke up.

"Thank you Lawerence. I will be sure that Samantha is assigned to tier two, so you will be able to keep an eye on her," the leader said.

"So, explain how our tiers mesh with the disciple tiers," Jerry inquired.

"I am having Sharon create a list for each disciples guard that is the head of the three tiers. They will know which disciples guard and disciples they are responsible for. Also, each of the disciples guard in the tiers will also be personally responsible for some of the disciples. I will have Sharon get each of the disciples guard a list of what disciples they are responsible for. That will, in a sense, make nine sub tiers. I want to make sure that each disciple feels that they have a personal disciples guard they can go to for the chain of command," Azril explained.

"Are we able to request specific disciples we want in our tier?" Jerry wondered.

"What do you mean by that? Is there a certain disciple you have your eyes on as a potential connected partner?" Azril asked Jerry.

"It is possible. There is one disciple I have been talking to, but I don't know how they feel about me. I was just thinking if they were assigned to me, maybe we could get closer," Jerry told Azril.

"Cory has Debora in his tier and directly assigned to him. Danny has Sara in his tier and directly assigned to him. Lawerence, you will get Samantha assigned to you and I have heard rumblings about Martin and Farrah, so they will be assigned together. Jerry, if there is a disciple you want assigned to you in order to get closer to, you need to speak up before the lists are made," Azril mentioned.

Jerry lowered his head and blushed. "Well, the disciple was involved in a bad break up and I don't want to force them into something, but it's Howard."

"Jerry, is that why you have never been in a relationship with someone that you allowed to meet us?" Lawerence asked.

"Both you and Walter would bring home potential partners, but I didn't know how you would feel about my lifestyle," Jerry admitted.

"This seems like a family discussion. Jerry, I will do what I can about placing Howard in your tier, as well as directly assigned to you. Other than that, Beatrice needs to be left alone for reflection. Let's head up and join the other disciples," Azril told them as they headed back up to the surface.

Twenty Nine

When all of the disciples gathered for nightly worship, Omegra assisted Emma with issuing the uniforms to any disciples who didn't have one. There were several disciples who had contributed to the City of Disciples that still hadn't acquired their uniforms.

Omegra stood in front of the worship area to address the disciples. "The uniform you have been issued corresponds with the beginner disciples. Once you relinquish your funds to the City of Disciples, this is the uniform each disciple receives. At this time, we are adding an area for God's cleanse in order to move you up to the dark blue uniform. We are aware that some of you are able to move up to level one, so those disciples will skip the dark blue uniforms and go directly to the green uniforms. We are also looking to get a large van that can fit at least ten disciples in. That won't include the disciples guard who is driving and the navigator disciple in the passenger seat. So, those of you who have relinquished your funds and still have a vehicle, we are requesting that you allow us to trade in your vehicles to get the van for the City of Disciples."

Sara stood up. "What about those of us who believe we should move up to level two? I believe there are a couple of us who should get the orange uniform."

"Sara, Debora and Sharon, we are aware of the dedication you have committed to the City of Disciples. We will be speaking to the three of you privately," Omegra explained.

Azril held his hands out over all the disciples to issue a group blessing. "I do have a temporary God's cleanse area set up for anyone who is ready. If you believe you are ready for God's cleanse, please stand up."

All of the disciples guard along with three quarters of the disciples stood. Azril led those that were standing, out of the worship area and over to the water trough that everyone had been using to wash in. The leader had the water drained and replaced with clean water in order to perform God's cleanse ceremony.

"Line up and we will get started with the God's cleanse," Azril instructed. "I want to make sure each of you understands that you have to recite the evil acts as listed in the Disciples Doctrine. Is everyone ready for that?"

As Omegra led the rest of the disciples out of the worship area in order to witness God's cleanse, some of the disciples that were in line, decided to leave the line and rejoin the other disciples. Omegra joined Azril, after the disciples took their seats to witness the ceremony.

Azril stood at one end of the trough. "I appreciate those of you who understand you aren't ready. If you aren't familiar with the God's cleanse chapter in the Disciples Doctrine, please read through it, so you are able to participate in the ceremony and begin recruiting outsiders."

Omegra stepped up next to the leader and addressed the disciples. "Those of you with vehicles here in the City of Disciples, please come see me after God's cleanse."

Azril moved around behind the water trough, in order to face the disciples. Before beginning the ceremony, the leader quietly said a prayer. He wanted to connect with God before addressing the disciples for God's cleanse.

The leader outstretched his arms, palms facing the disciples in line for God's cleanse. "We are joined here together today for these disciples to wash away their old life and emerge into their new life as a Disciple of God. God's cleanse is meant to fill these disciples with righteous indignation to feel God enter their soul. Once they are cleansed, they are expected to live within favor of God. After the cleanse is completed, each disciple is guaranteed a place in the promised land with God."

The leader slowly lowered his arms, gently placed his hand on the back of the first disciple's neck and dunked their head into the water. Once the disciple stood back up, they ran their hands through their hair, smoothing it back, then recited the evil acts, before stepping to the other side of Azril. One by one, each disciple stepped up, dunked their head and recited the evil acts.

Once the last disciple in line had completed God's cleanse, the leader addressed everyone in the City of Disciples. "Join with me in reciting the God's Cleanse prayer. I bring to you my God, these disciples into the family of God. They are ready to join us here in the City of Disciples and are cleansing their old life out, as well as accepting their new life with You in their heart. We thank You for the promised land where we are meant to go once we are released from the physical land. We are Disciples of God and we will appease You in worship."

"We are Disciples of God and we will appease You in worship," the disciples all repeated in unison.

Azril addressed all the disciples. "Those of you who have just been cleansed, please see Emma. She is standing in the back of the crowd, ready to trade your light blue uniform for the dark blue. The disciples guard has all been cleansed as well, but they are all in the grey uniforms. Now then, any of the cleansed disciples, if you have been talking to any other disciple and would like to learn more about becoming connected partners, please join me and my connected partner in the worship area once you are dismissed. I appreciate each and every one of you for witnessing the God's cleanse. When the rest of you are ready and know the evil acts that should not be committed here in the City of Disciples, I will be encouraging you to approach after each worship service.

"I appreciate you taking the time to listen to

this very important message that God has spoken through me. I am a Disciple of God and I will appease Him in worship."

"I am a Disciple of God and I will appease Him in worship," all of the disciples repeated, before dispersing to their evening job assignments.

Several of the disciples guard met up with other disciples, before heading into the worship area, in the center of the circle of housing tents. Omegra met up with Azril over near the water trough where he was dishing out blessings to the disciples who were thanking him for God's cleanse.

"Let Sara, Debora and Sharon know that I want to see them after I talk to the couples," Azril told Omegra.

"They are all in there with Cory, Danny and Walter, so you will get a chance to talk to them," Omegra said, kissing him on his cheek.

Once all the disciples were gone, the leader and his connected partner headed over to the worship area. All of the couples were conversing and seemed very happy together.

Azril stepped in front of his housing tent, as the couples were facing that direction. "In order to become connected partners, disciples must request connected studies from the leader. Connected studies is a specified class for partners to participate in. It will determine compatibility and whether you are committed to each other as well as the City of Disciples. Disciples must be sure their partner is the one single disciple they want to be connected to on the physical land as well as when they are released into the promised land, to which God will reunite them."

Cory interjected. "Is there a limit as to who can and cannot be connected partners in the eyes of God?"

Azril shook his head. "Connected partners come in all different shapes, styles and colors and there isn't a single difference between them. As a Disciple of God, we are all accepting to every connected partner of every different type. No matter who you choose as your connected partner in the physical land, God will accept you and reunite the two of you, when you are released into the promised land."

Omegra spoke up. "In other words, if two disciples feel as though they have been brought together by God, then God approves of their connection."

Azril nodded and wrapped his arm around his connected partner's waist. "If any of you today would like to participate in connected studies, please feel free to sign up with Omegra. I would like to speak with Sara, Debora and Sharon on a separate matter. Cory, Danny and Walter, if y'all are ready for connected studies, the three of you can sign up while I speak with your partners."

As the three disciples stood to go with Azril, Cory, Danny, Martin, Walter, Lawerence and Jerry all stepped up to join Omegra. Martin was there with Farrah, Lawerence was there with Samantha and Jerry was there with Howard.

Thirty

Omegra spoke to the six partners who were interested in participating in connected studies, as Azril took the three disciples over to see Emma. He wanted to reward the disciples for their hard work and dedication they have shown to the City of Disciples.

Azril stopped right outside of Emma's housing tent. "You three have brought the most disciples into the City of Disciples. Now that you have participated in God's cleanse, I would like to extend my appreciation by trading out those dark blue uniforms with the proper uniform you are owed, along with the proper pay. Sharon, with the five you brought in recently, you can trade out for orange. Sara and Debora, I understand y'all have been trying to get closer to Cory and Danny, but you are able to move up to green."

"I appreciate the recognition, Leader and agree with your assessment," Sara said.

"Thank you, Leader," Debora acknowledged.

"I trust you, as the leader of the disciples, that God has chosen the right person to spread the message as told in the Disciples Doctrine," Sharon said.

Azril nodded, then gave each one of them a blessing. "Emma, are you in?"

Emma poked her head out of the opening of her tent. "Yes, Leader. Omegra informed me that you would be stopping by to level up a few disciples."

Azril placed his hand on Emma's head. "Thank you, Emma. We have one Orange and two Green."

Azril left the three disciples with Emma, as he headed back to his housing tent. Omegra was still talking to the disciples about the connected studies. Sean and Cora had joined the others. Azril had seen them schmoozing, but didn't realize they were getting close enough to request connected studies.

"I want to be sure that each and every one of you have discussed connection with each other," Azril said, as he stepped up next to Omegra.

When Debora returned, dressed in her new green uniform, she approached Cory and cuddled up into him. Sara returned in her new green uniform and approached Danny. She grabbed his hand and giggled. Martin and Farrah were leaning against each other, shoulder to shoulder. Jerry and Howard were sitting, facing each other, interlocking their fingers together and flirting. Sharon returned, dressed in her new orange uniform and danced up to Walter on her tip toes. Sean and Cora were just sitting next to each other, with one of their knees touching the other.

David entered the worship area and stepped up next to the leader, with his back to the couples. "The police are here again. It is the same two as before."

Azril nodded, as David walked away. "There is a situation I need to deal with. Please feel free to be sure you know each other enough in order to become connected partners. I will be back as soon as this is taken care of."

Azril left the worship area, as Omegra stayed behind and the couples continued talking to each other. The leader met up with David and the two of them approached the two officers.

The leader extended his arm to shake hands with the police. "Officer Juarez and Romero. What brings you by?"

"There is a car that has been abandoned up on the roadside," Officer Romero informed.

"I'm sorry. Everyone here on the property has parked their vehicles here away from the roadway. I'm sure it doesn't belong to anyone here," Azril told them.

"The car is registered to someone who has been reported missing. Do you know anything about that?" Officer Juarez asked.

Azril shook his head. "No sir. If you tell me their name, I could confirm if they are here."

"The name is Lonny Anderson," Romero told him, looking down at the notepad in his hand.

"We have approximately twenty two hundred people here on the property, but I can guarantee we don't have anyone by that name. You are welcome to go around and speak to everyone if you would like," the leader offered.

Juarez shook his head and nudged Romero with his elbow. "That's okay. Thank you for your time. We are going to tow the vehicle and get it off the road."

Azril again extended his arm to shake hands with the officers. "No problem. If you need us to keep an eye out for any suspicious activity, I will be sure to assign someone to watch out for that."

"You mentioned the last time we were here about building a wall around the property. Once the wall is set up, I'm sure you will be secure back here and you most likely won't see us again," Romero said, as they both walked back to the police cruiser.

Azril turned toward David, as the officers drove off the property. "I need you and Stephen to guard the front entrance. If anymore outsiders are able to get onto this property in order to inflict pain upon the disciples, the disciples guard will start paying for it. I will assign six others to swap out with you, for a total of four daily shifts. Until we get the wall and entrance gate put up, I want the City of Disciples to be all unicorns and rainbows."

Before David could respond, Azril walked away and headed toward the worship area. All the couples seemed to be having a great time. The leader stepped up to his connected partner and kissed her on the cheek.

Omegra tilted her head. "Is everything okay?"

Azril nodded. "Lonny's car was found at the road in front of the property. He was reported missing, but he can't be connected to us."

"Thank goodness for that," Omegra said.

Azril took a deep breath and cleared his throat to the couple's attention. "Lawerence and Samantha, I think the two of you might benefit more with private bible study with Omegra, as well as Sean and Cora before going through connected studies. Your partnership is still new and you need to be sure that y'all are compatible with each other. Also, Jerry and Howard, the two of you are a little too new to confirm as being connected partners."

Omegra ushered the three new couples - Lawerence and Samantha, Sean and Cora, Jerry and Howard - into the sunroom of the tent, while Azril stayed in the worship area in order to discuss the connected studies class with the others - Cory and Debora, Danny and Sara, Martin and Farrah, Walter and Sharon.

The leader took a seat and had the couples create a circle. "For the next three weeks, we are going to talk about all of the things that come up during a relationship. When you are single, you only have to think about one person, yourself. Once you are connected partners, you then have to start thinking about the other person as well. Every activity you do, must be agreed upon between the two of you. If one of you is going to spend your free time doing something without your connected partner, your partner must also agree with what you are going to do, as there should never be any secrets between connected partners."

Danny raised his hand. "What do you mean that if one of us is going to do something without the other, the other has to agree with what we are doing?"

"Well, let's say the disciples guard is going to gather and just sit around. The twelve of you. Your connected partner must agree that it is okay for you to go sit around with just the disciples guard. It would mean that Sara also has something to do as well at the same time and she isn't feeling as though you are avoiding spending time with her," Azril answered.

"Basically, we should be either spending our free time with our connected partners, or making sure that they are okay with us spending our free time with other disciples?" Danny wondered.

Azril tilted his head. "Not exactly. It is more that your connected partner agrees that the other disciples you are going to be gathering with align with God's message and they don't think that you are going to be swayed to defect from the City of Disciples."

Cory raised his hand to add his two cents. "Also, you are suppose to share your secrets with your connected partner. That means that you are telling them exactly where you are going to be and who you are going to be with."

Azril nodded in agreement. "That is exactly right, Cory. Plus, when you get back from whatever you were doing, you are to communicate with your connected partner. Communication is the foundation to a happy and long lasting partnership. Separation between connected partners on the physical land, is only allowed if the leader agrees to the separation after both of the connected partners have stated their reasons for the separation."

"What if you don't agree to the separation?" Cory wondered.

The leader pressed the palms of his hands together and rested his chin on the tips of his middle fingers. "The two of you will be assigned to a two room temporary housing tent. You are to do everything together throughout the time that you are assigned to stay in that tent. I will join you once a day to discuss anything y'all are disagreeing on. If you can rediscover the reasons you wanted to become connected partners in the first place, then I have done my job, if not, then the separation will commence."

Sara playfully shoved Cory. "Are you already looking to find out how to get out of our connection if we don't work out?"

Cory wrapped his arms around her shoulders and pulled her in to kiss her cheek. "No, I just want to know in case someone else asks me about it because it is mentioned in the Disciples Doctrine."

Omegra and the other disciples emerged from the leader's housing tent. The couples were clutching each other and smiling. Azril's connected partner approached him and placed her hands on his shoulders.

"What do you think about those three couples? Are they ready for connected studies?" Azril asked her.

"I think that once they have gone through the connected studies with you, they should be ready," Omegra told him.

Azril stood up as all seven couples awaited his assessment. "Okay, to those of you who have just joined us, I think I'm going to continue the connected studies with only two couples for now. These two couples have been getting to know each other since the beginning. After the three weeks is done with them, they will go through the connection ceremony and then I will start connected studies with two more couples."

"Cory and Danny have been together Debora and Sara since you were preaching at the college.

I can understand why they get to go first. I'm okay with waiting. That just means I get to find out more about Sharon," Walter said.

Jerry linked one arm with Howard and rubbed the palm of his hand on his partner's upper arm. "I understand. We need to make sure that we know the person we are going to be connected to, before we are connected for the entirety of our time here on the physical land."

Azril nodded his head. "Exactly. Is everyone okay with that decision?"

Sean linked his arm with Cora. "God speaks through you and you are the one who knows what God wants us to do. We trust you, as the leader of the physical land, to guide us through God's message, as it is the way into the promised land."

The five new couples left the worship area, leaving the leader and his connected partner with Cory, Debora, Danny and Sara. Azril and Omegra sat down with the disciples.

They were sure they were ready for the connected ceremony, but each couple had to go through connected studies with the leader. For the two head disciples guard and their partners, Azril wanted to see how well they would work together as a team.

It was time to begin building the permanent housing structure, as well as the medical building.

C. L. Conolly

The Disciples of God were a strong group and they were only getting started.

About the Author

C. L. Conolly is an avid horror and true crime fan. Her novels are meant to bring attention to real world issues with a major gore focus. She attends several horror conventions and events each year in order to meet readers in person. To find out more, check out www.clconolly.com and follow on all social media platforms.

When C. L. Conolly isn't writing, she's relaxing at her country home with her husband, family and pets. She has one son, a daughter-in-law and two grandchildren.

Facebook - C. L. Conolly - Author
Instagram - C. L. Conolly
Twitter - @CLConolly
TikTok - @c.l.conolly
YouTube - @c.l.conolly